MW00414790

SWEET LOVE AND DEVOTION

A SWEET COVE MYSTERY BOOK 14

J. A. WHITING

Copyright 2018 J.A. Whiting

Cover copyright 2018 Susan Coils at www.coverkicks.com

Formatting by Signifer Book Design

Proofreading by Donna Rich

This book is a work of fiction. Names, characters, places, or incidents are products of the author's imagination or are used fictitiously. Any resemblance to locales, actual events, or persons, living or dead, is entirely coincidental.

All rights reserved.

No part of this publication can be reproduced or transmitted in any form or by any means, electronic or mechanical, without permission in writing from J. A. Whiting.

To hear about new books and book sales, please sign up for my mailing list at:

www.jawhitingbooks.com

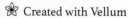 Created with Vellum

For my family with love
And to my readers with grateful appreciation

1

The last of the day's April light filtered into the attic through the small round window at the front of the Victorian mansion and sent a golden ray over the scuffed wood floor. Euclid, the Roseland family's big orange cat sat in the warmth of the sunbeam as it illuminated the different shades of orange and white in his fur and made him look like he was glowing. Circe, the small black cat with a white patch on her chest, had settled in the light behind Euclid with her paws tucked under her body making her shape resemble a loaf.

Angie walked around the space looking for something and when she ducked under a beam, her honey-blond ponytail swung into a spider's web causing her to brush her hand over the strands to remove the piece of sticky gray-white web. "Bah."

The oldest Roseland sister hadn't been up in the attic for months and although she had something specific in mind to find, she enjoyed strolling around and admiring the old pieces of furniture, artwork, and boxes that had been left to her by a distant relative who once owned the mansion.

Her youngest sister, Courtney, was working at her Main Street candy shop; Ellie, the tall blond middle sister, was downstairs checking in a new guest to the inn; and Jenna, Angie's twin, was finishing up in her jewelry shop at the rear of the house so she could join her sister in the attic soon.

Walking to peek out of the round window, Angie looked down at the front lawn and the street that ran past the house and down to the beach. A few people walked by on their way to the ocean and others headed up the road to the center of town to the stores and restaurants. Looking down from the high perch at the top of the mansion always gave Angie a twinge of vertigo, but she loved looking out over the treetops of the little seaside town of Sweet Cove. When she lifted her hand to shield her eyes from the glare of the setting sun, the diamond on her engagement ring caught the light and sparkled. It was hard to believe, but it was only six weeks to the wedding day when she and her fiancé, Josh Williams, would say *I do*.

"You up here, Angie?" Jenna called from the skinny staircase.

"By the window," she said to her sister.

Circe trilled and went to meet the tall, brunette who resembled her fraternal twin not in height or coloring, but in similar facial features and mannerisms.

"Did you find it?" Jenna asked as she stepped into the attic and glanced around with a smile. "This space is like a treasure trove. Imagine if we lived in this house when we were growing up? We would have spent hours and hours playing up here. Mom wouldn't have been able to drag us out."

"I know. I love this attic." Angie smiled and bent to scratch Euclid's head. "And, no, I haven't found it yet." Walking past some old sailor's chests, she added, "Are we even sure it's up here? Maybe we put it in the storage area of the carriage house."

"Ellie said it's up here," Jenna informed her twin. "We just have to find it amidst all this stuff." Lifting a box and setting it down behind her, she said, "The wedding is coming fast. It will be here before you know it."

Angie was rummaging through an old armoire when she stood straight. "Josh and I have had a lot of fun planning the details, but we're both ready now. It's time." She looked over at her sister. "I can't believe I found someone like Josh."

"He's the best," Jenna said. "But if we don't find this box, you might have to walk down the aisle naked."

Euclid hissed at Jenna's joke, but Angie said with a chuckle, "I don't think it will come to that. I'm sure I could find something to wear." A few seconds later, she let out a whistle. "Here it is." Her voice was excited as she carried the large box to the center of the attic and set it down on a rug in the middle of the floor.

The rectangular box had a plastic front in which to see the bodice of the cleaned and preserved white wedding gown.

Jenna knelt next to the box. "Look how pretty it is."

Angie touched her finger to the plastic. "It sure is. I always thought Mom looked like a princess in her wedding day photos."

"Shall we open it?" Jenna looked to her twin.

Angie took a deep breath and shook her head. "Why am I so nervous about this?"

Jenna reached over and gave her sister a hug. "It's a big deal. If it fits you ... well, this is going to be your wedding gown."

"Okay," Angie whispered. "Let's open it. Did you bring the pocket knife?"

"Right here." Jenna held up the small knife in a red case. "This is my first duty as a maid of honor."

"Matron of honor. You're married," Angie corrected.

"Right." Jenna frowned. "But that word. *Matron*. It sounds like some old hag."

With a chuckle, Angie said, "Maybe we can come up with a different title for you."

Jenna flipped the blade from its case and moved it slowly around the edge of the box to break the seal, and then Angie carefully lifted the lid.

"Wow. It's pure white still," Jenna marveled and carefully touched the lace at the edge of the neckline. "It's beautiful. Let's take it downstairs so you can try it on."

Before Angie could answer, Euclid let out a low growl from deep in his chest.

"What's wrong with him?" Jenna looked over to see the cat sitting on an old wooden desk.

Angie lifted her eyes and followed her sister's gaze. "He seems off this evening." She made eye contact with Jenna. "Have you felt anything ... funny, today?"

The smile fell from the brunette's face when she asked, "Funny, how?"

"You know what I mean," Angie told her and nervously pushed a strand of hair from her forehead.

"Not really. Well, maybe I felt a little something." Jenna narrowed her eyes. "Have you?"

Angie sat down next to the box they'd just opened. "A little. I guess more than a little."

"There hasn't been any trouble since Christmas," Jenna noted. "We're due."

The corner of Angie's mouth turned down. "Couldn't trouble wait another six weeks so we could get through the wedding?"

"Maybe it's nothing. A false alarm probably." Jenna made an attempt at being hopeful, but really? She'd felt something strange on the air for a few days. "Have you asked Mr. Finch if he's noticed anything?"

"Not yet." Angie ran her hand gently over her mother's wedding dress. "I've been thinking a lot about Mom."

"Have you?"

Angie gave a little nod. "Why do you think she never shows up?"

Jenna's heart began to race. The four Roseland sisters each had a few *special* skills. One of Jenna's talents was that she could see ghosts.

"Do you ever wonder why sometimes Nana shows up, but Mom never does?" Angie asked.

"I guess I haven't." Jenna wrinkled her forehead in thought. "It never crossed my mind. Maybe because we know Nana had the same skills we all have, but we aren't sure about Mom."

Circe padded over to Angie and settled in the young woman's lap.

"I think Mom had abilities, but like Ellie, she had a hard time accepting them," Angie said.

"I think you're right. She didn't want anything to do with *special* skills."

Years ago, the Roseland sisters' mother had been hit by a car while crossing a Boston street and was killed.

With the setting of the sun, the attic had darkened despite a few lamps being on in the space. Something red flashed outside the window and Angie looked over to it.

A reddish stream of light came in through the

windowpane, ran along the walls like the strobe of a lighthouse beam, and then disappeared.

"What was that?" Jenna walked with purpose to the window, but Euclid beat her to it. He jumped up on a high dusty armoire, flicked his tail, and peered out through the window.

"What do you see, Euclid?" When Jenna saw what was outside, she turned back to her sister without saying anything, and just stood there.

Angie stood up and dusted off her butt. "Shall we go downstairs?"

"It's Chief Martin," Jenna said softly.

"I thought so." Angie picked up the box that held her mother's wedding gown.

"Why did you think so?"

"The red light that came in. I figured it was the light on the top of his cruiser."

"It could have been from something else." When Jenna started away from the window, Euclid leapt down and raced for the staircase with Circe right behind him.

"No, it couldn't." Angie's voice was resigned. "Let's go see what's wrong."

The sisters moved carefully down the narrow stairs to the third floor of the Victorian, passed the door to Angie's and Josh's new apartment, and headed down the two beautifully carved staircases towards the first floor.

"Angie. Jenna." Ellie called to her sisters from the foyer. "Chief Martin just pulled up out front." When the cats raced from the stairs into the foyer and to the front door, Ellie shrugged a shoulder. "Oh. I guess they know he's here."

Opening the front door, Ellie greeted Chief Phillip Martin, a tall, stocky man in his late-fifties.

He removed his hat. "Evening, Ellie."

The cats sat next to Ellie waiting for the chief to come inside.

"Come in." Ellie stepped back to let the man enter. "It's a lovely night." Catching herself, her face clouded and she tentatively asked a question. "*Is* it a lovely night?"

The chief leaned down to pat the cats, and Euclid turned his face up to sniff the air. "It was ... up until about an hour ago."

With the big box encircled by Angie's arms, she and Jenna stood at the bottom of the staircase, their blue eyes trained on Chief Martin.

"We were in the attic. We saw you drive up," Jenna said. "Is everything okay?"

Angie tilted her head slightly to the side. "You smell like smoke."

"Do I?" The chief asked, only slightly surprised. "There's a reason for that." The big man sighed. "Care to have a chat?"

No, Angie did not want to have a chat, but the family would do anything to help Chief Martin, and knowing they were about to be drawn into something, she tightened her arms around the box and made a silent wish that she sent out into the world.

Please don't let anything happen to any of us.

2

Angie, Jenna, Ellie, Chief Martin and the two cats had just entered the family room at the back of the house when they heard the youngest Roseland sister call out from the hall.

"Where is everyone?" Courtney walked into the room with Mr. Finch right behind her, carrying a rectangular box. About the same height as Angie and with the same honey-blond hair, Courtney and her older sister looked more alike than the two twins did. "Here you are," she said when she saw her sisters and the chief sitting on the sofas and chairs. "What's cookin'? Having a pow-wow without me and Mr. Finch?"

Holding his cane in one hand, Mr. Finch care-

11

fully placed the box on the coffee table. "Miss Courtney and I have been making some new sweets and thought we could have a taste-test." Finch glanced around at the others over the tops of his black-rimmed eyeglasses and noticed the somber looking faces. "Perhaps the taste-testing will need to wait?"

Victor Finch was an older man who had come to Sweet Cove to track down his mean and hateful brother, but the nasty Mr. Finch had been murdered that very day in his candy store. The good Finch inherited the business and became close to the sisters who "adopted" him into their family. Finch tapped Courtney to be his partner and the two built the sweet shop into one of the most popular stores in town.

"I know *I* can talk and eat at the same time," the chief said. "It's been a heck of an evening. Some sweets would hit the spot right now, and I'd be happy to give my opinion on the new items."

Still wearing the apron from the candy shop, Courtney sat in the easy chair next to Euclid and swung her legs over the arm of the chair. "So what's wrong? I felt something this morning, but I thought trouble would take some time to find us."

"You felt uneasy?" Angie asked, relieved that

other family members were experiencing odd sensations. "Have you felt anything?" she asked Mr. Finch.

Finch let out a long sigh as Circe crawled onto the older man's lap. "Indeed, I have. With the approaching wedding, I hoped the feelings would pass by and go elsewhere. It seems my wish will not come true." He turned his gaze to Chief Martin. "What seems to be the issue?"

"May I?" the chief gestured to the candy box and lifted the lid after Finch gave a nod. Selecting a fancy chocolate, he bit into it, closed his eyes, and let out a soft moan. "You'll have to move the box, otherwise I'll eat them all." The chief sat up and cleared his throat. "You've heard there have been two fires in the Park River neighborhood of Silver Cove?"

Nods went around the room. Park River hugged the coast where Silver Cove met Sweet Cove.

"There was a third fire tonight. Another single family house. Pretty badly damaged."

"It's definitely arson then," Jenna said.

"Yes. The fire investigator agreed that the two previous fires had been set and then with the third event this evening, that sealed the deal. Silver Cove is being menaced by an arsonist. A very prolific arsonist."

"Three fires in what? Five days?" Angie asked.

"That's right. And we don't think he'll be stopping at three." The chief reached for another chocolate. "These are delicious, by the way."

"It's April," Ellie said. "The tourist season will kick into high gear soon. The area can't have a firebug running around causing trouble. Tourists will go elsewhere." Ellie's eyes widened. "No one was hurt tonight, right?"

"The couple who lived in the house got out just in time," the chief said. "Accelerant was not used, but the place was fully engulfed in minutes. The couple was very fortunate to escape."

"It's lucky no one has been hurt," Angie rubbed at the tension in her forehead.

"Was accelerant used at any of the houses?" Courtney asked.

"None was used at the first two homes. The investigator will need some time to determine the cause in this case, however, we believe the three fires are related and were likely set by the same person."

"Why would someone do this?" Ellie fiddled with the end of a strand of her long blond hair.

"That question is often very difficult to answer when dealing with crimes," Finch said. "For whatever reason, something gets triggered in a person's brain and trouble begins. Anger at someone, perceived slights or hurts, feelings of depression or abandonment or being unloved can all set someone off. Perhaps there is a predisposition to react unreasonably or strongly. Someone else could go through a similar situation and not turn to crime. A psychologist or psychiatrist would have more insight, but even then, some actions are unexplainable."

"Is arson harder to solve than other crimes?" Courtney asked.

The chief squared his shoulders and gave a nod. "Only about fifteen percent of arson cases result in an arrest and only two percent close with a conviction."

"Why so few convictions?" Angie asked.

"Because the evidence is destroyed in the fire or is significantly altered by the fire," Chief Martin said. "There is often very little to go on." He raised his hands, palm up, in a helpless gesture.

"Are the houses that were set on fire close to each other?" Jenna asked.

"Not really," the chief said. "They're in the same neighborhood, but not on the same street and there is no discernible pattern to the fires."

"Do the people who live in the burned homes have any connections to one another?" Angie's eyes had widened.

"That's still being looked into."

Ellie asked with a tremor in her voice, "Did you come here to ask us to get involved?"

"It would be a big help," the chief said.

"Good," Courtney told him with excitement in her eyes. "We haven't had a crime to solve since Christmas. We're getting out of practice. Mr. Finch and I have watched some crime shows about arson so we have some background."

Ellie made a face. "Watching a television show doesn't actually give you experience or credentials, you know."

"It gives us ideas. It's helped with cases in the past." Courtney patted Euclid and the big cat purred loudly, but continued to listen to the discussion that was going on. "Well, let's get cracking. Angie's getting married in a few weeks. We need to have this solved by then."

The corners of the chief's mouth turned up at the young woman's energy and positive outlook. "Remember to carry your official police department ID's with you while you're working on the case." The chief had made the family official Sweet Cove police consultants and presented them with the necessary identifications at Christmas time.

"I carry mine with me all the time," Courtney smiled. "Now we finally have a reason to use them."

"Just don't mention to people about the paranormal powers," Ellie warned.

"Don't worry, sis. I know the drill." Courtney moved the orange cat to the side and stood up. "So what do you want us to do first?"

"If you're able, I'd like all of you to come to the scene of the fire and have a look," Chief Martin said. "We can't get close, of course, but we can stand on the sidewalk and maybe, well, you know, maybe you can pick up on things?"

For years, the Roseland sisters' nana had worked with the police helping on cases, and Chief Martin, despite not understanding how paranormal things worked, respected and understood the value of such abilities. The man was not the least bit surprised that the sisters and Mr. Finch had some *talents*.

"Now? You want us to come tonight?" Angie asked glancing over at the box with her mother's wedding dress inside.

"I thought it could be helpful," the chief said.

"Great," Courtney said. "But before we go, everyone needs to try some of the new candies and give me and Mr. Finch your opinions. We've been working hard on these chocolates. It will only take a few minutes and the burned down house isn't going anywhere." Courtney lifted the box and passed the sweets around to the family. "And while you're sampling, I'm going to text Rufus and tell him we're on a new case."

It only took several minutes for the taste-testers to sample the new confections, give their opinions, and select their favorites. There were three clear winners and Courtney and Mr. Finch decided to put those into the store's rotation.

Everyone went to get their jackets or sweaters to make the short, fifteen-minute trip to the fire-affected neighborhood of Silver Cove.

Angie kept her voice down when she asked Mr. Finch, "How do you feel about the case? Will it be dangerous?"

Finch stood leaning on his cane in the foyer waiting for the others to assemble. "It's hard to say, Miss Angie. I've felt it coming for us for some time. We'll need to be on our guard."

"It makes me nervous. I don't know why exactly. Maybe because of the carriage house fire," Angie said.

The carriage house behind the Victorian had been set on fire over a year ago by someone who wanted to kill Angie and her sisters. The sights, sounds, and smells of the terrible night and the young women's subsequent escape from the burning building had had a strong impact on Angie and she shuddered thinking about having to investigate an arson case.

"Unfortunately, the night of that fire is burned into my memory," Finch said with a slow shake of his head, "and I will never forget it. I thought I had lost you." The man's eyes watered. "Maybe because of that experience, we will be better equipped to handle this case successfully."

Angie slid her arm through Finch's. "That's one of the things I love about you, Mr. Finch. Ever the optimist."

"It's the only way forward, Miss Angie." Finch tapped his cane lightly on the rug. "And we shall move forward, all of us together."

Euclid and Circe, sitting by the front door waiting to go along with the family to Silver Cove, trilled their approval.

3

Police Chief Martin parked his cruiser next to the curb and Ellie pulled her van in right behind him. Everyone was quiet on the ride to the crime scene, each person thinking about the fires that had been set.

The sisters piled out of the van and Courtney assisted Mr. Finch by taking his arm and holding his cane for him until he emerged from the vehicle and had steadied himself. With two windows cracked, the cats sat on the front seat of the van watching the activities going on at the burned house.

"Fire can leave behind a foul odor," Finch said. "Burned wood, an unpleasant chemical smell, an acrid, bitter stench in the air."

Courtney took the man's arm. "It reminds me of the carriage house fire."

Finch nodded in agreement.

"Stay here, kitties," Angie told the cats. "If it's safe for you to come out, we'll come back and get you."

Up ahead, firefighters and officials moved around the outside of the house while others went in and out through the front door. The sides and back walls of the home were scorched black. Part of the roof had caved in and windows had been shattered either by the intense heat of the blaze or by the work of the firefighters. Some trees close to the left of the house had been damaged by the inferno and were dark and scary looking with their ruined limbs hanging down at odd angles.

Nodding to his colleagues as he walked past, the chief led the small group of consultants along the sidewalk across from the home and when they were directly in front, he stopped.

"This is as close as we can get. It's too dark to get much more done tonight, but the investigators need to get photographs and make detailed notes about what they see and find. It will take a while and then they'll return very early in the morning."

"You said a couple lived in the house?" Jenna asked.

"That's right. They're in their late twenties. They moved in two years ago. It was their first house. They lost everything, all their belongings."

"Where are they now?" Ellie asked.

"They're going to stay with the young woman's sister in Sweet Cove. The sister lives down near Coveside. We can arrange to have you speak with the couple, if you think it would help."

"I'd like to speak with them." Angie's eyes roved over the scene ... the people hustling back and forth, the house that looked like something from a horror movie, the charred vegetation. She moved down the sidewalk to get a look towards the rear of the property. "It's wooded behind the house. Easy for someone to sneak into the yard undetected."

"What's behind the house?" Courtney asked. "Is there another home on the other side of the trees?"

"This house's land goes all the way over to the next street," the chief said.

"Convenient," Finch said. "Once into the woods, the perpetrator would be concealed as he approached the house."

"And it was dark out, too," Jenna noted. "Lots of trees and shadows to hide the person."

"What about the two other houses that have been burned?" Angie asked. "Are there lots of trees around them? Are there neighbors on both sides?"

"This was the easiest house to target because of the privacy afforded by the setting of the large lot," the chief said. "The first house has neighbors on both sides, but there are some trees in between the lots. The second house was set back from the road with evergreens lining the driveway. It's visible from the street, but there are plenty of trees on the property to give someone cover."

"Who owns the other two houses?" Mr. Finch questioned.

Chief Martin pulled up the notes on his phone. "The first targeted home is owned by a couple named Benson, in their late-fifties. Kids are grown. They owned the house for about thirty years. The second place is owned by a man in his early sixties, divorced, no kids. Bennington is his last name. He's lived in the house for a little more than ten years."

"No obvious connection between the owners?" Jenna asked.

"Nothing that jumps out," the chief said. "That's still being investigated though."

"Are the Bensons and Mr. Bennington still in the

area?" Angie asked. "Are they available to speak with?"

"The Bensons are staying with some friends one town over and Mr. Bennington has taken a suite in the Sweet Cove resort for now. I'll make arrangements with them to meet with you."

"Did any of them hear or see anything suspicious on the nights of the fires?" Finch asked.

"Mr. Bennington reported hearing some kind of rustling sounds outside. He was in his den at the back of the house, his window was open. Bennington thought nothing of the sound at the time, he thought it was a strong wind in the trees."

Courtney scrunched up her face. "Wind in the trees? A rustling sound? I don't know."

Five faces turned her way.

"What do you mean?" Ellie asked.

"The leaves aren't even out yet, only buds." Courtney looked up and down the dark street at the trees. "How do leafless trees make a rustling sound?"

"Excellent observation, Miss Courtney," Finch said.

"See. Watching all those crime shows makes me and Mr. Finch more aware of stuff. Right, Mr. Finch?"

"Most definitely."

"We'll need to question Mr. Bennington about what he heard," Courtney said. "Ask him to carefully describe the sound to us."

"None of these victims have an enemy?" Ellie asked.

"They did not believe they had any enemies," the chief said.

"Did any of them have suspicions about who might have set their home on fire?" Angie questioned.

"They couldn't think of anyone who would do such a thing." Chief Martin noticed one of the officers waving him over. "I'll be right back. Why don't you ... you know, um, see what you can pick up on?"

When the chief crossed the street, Mr. Finch suggested they spread out along the sidewalk in order to better concentrate so Courtney and Ellie moved to the left and Angie and Jenna walked to the right.

When Angie closed her eyes to clear her mind, the smell of the burned building was especially pungent and it nearly turned her stomach. Taking deep breaths and trying to block out the sounds of law enforcement buzzing around the crime scene, Angie felt her muscles begin to relax. When the light breeze pushed against her, it was as if something other than the wind was passing by. What was it? What did she feel?

Confusion ... chaos ... a thrill from being the cause of the havoc and tumult.

The sensation was so disturbing that Angie's heart began to race and her eyes popped open.

"Jenna?" Angie looked a few yards to her right. Her twin walked over to her.

"Did you feel anything?" Jenna asked. She had her hands shoved into the pockets of her jacket.

"Something weird. Like someone was getting a high from setting the fire."

Jenna nodded. "I felt darkness, and delight from causing the trouble."

Angie asked, "Did you see anything? Any images? A face?" There were times at crime scenes when Jenna was able to see a victim or a perpetrator move across a room.

"No, nothing like that. I just picked up on some sensations." Jenna glanced around the street and over at the burned home, and she shuddered. "The arsonist must be giving off very strong emotions if we both sensed similar things."

The young women walked over to Mr. Finch.

"Did you pick up on anything?" Angie asked the man.

Finch had both hands on the top of his cane and his face was serious. "This person ... the one who set the fire ... gives off a twisted sense of excitement. I feel it on the air. The person is so full of a sense of power and delight at what he has wrought that it seeps from his pores. It's very disturbing. The arsonist is not even close to being finished with his work."

"I detected the same things." Courtney approached from the left with Ellie at her side. "A sense of wild excitement. The air is full of it."

"How about you?" Angie asked Ellie. "Did you feel these same things?"

"I experienced something different." Ellie swallowed. "I felt ... revenge. It's very strong. It scares me."

"I also get the impression that this person is highly intelligent." Mr. Finch slowly rotated his cane under his palm and looked at each of the sisters. "This is going to be a difficult case."

Chief Martin walked towards them. "How did it go?"

The Roselands and Finch shared their sensations with the chief and his jaw twitched slightly when he heard the news.

"Not exactly what I'd hoped." The chief let out a

sigh. "But your sensations line up with research on arsonists. Forensic psychiatrists have determined that excitement and revenge are two of the motivations for arson."

"What are the other motivations besides those two?" Jenna asked.

"The others are concealment of a crime, vandalism, and terrorism."

"Those three reasons can probably be eliminated," Finch said.

"I agree," Chief Martin said.

"We believe this person will strike again," Finch told the chief.

Chief Martin's shoulders sagged. "Also something I hoped not to hear, but the news is expected."

A strange sensation moved over Angie's skin causing her to turn around abruptly.

A small, well-tended ranch-style house with a front porch stood next to the burned building. The overhead light shone down on an older woman and a man next to her. The man was in a wheelchair. The woman had her hand against her cheek and was staring over at Chief Martin.

The chief noticed the couple a few moments after Angie. "I think I'd better go talk to them. Maybe I can help set their minds at ease just a bit."

When Angie looked at the couple again, her vision flared red for a quick second and her breath caught in her throat. As her stomach tightened with anxiety, she blurted, "Tell the couple to leave their porch lights on all night. If there are outside lights on the back of the house, tell them to leave those on, too. Keep a lamp on in the living room."

Chief Martin stared at Angie. "Okay. Will do," he said.

Jenna took hold of her sister's arm and they all returned to Ellie's van for the ride home. "This isn't going to be easy."

4

In their late-fifties, Marta and Willy Benson met Angie and Courtney at the bake shop after the store had closed for the day. The couple didn't mind stopping in Sweet Cove to talk because they planned on heading to Silver Cove to meet with an insurance agent. Marta had short, dark blond hair and blue eyes, was slender and of average height. Her husband, Willy, was just under six feet tall, slim, with salt and pepper hair and blue eyes. They looked to be active people and exuded a pleasant energy.

With a beaming smile, Courtney produced her police badge and showed it to the couple and then Angie did the same.

"We're called in by the police occasionally to

conduct interviews and consult on cases," Angie explained. "We do the work on a part-time basis."

The Bensons accepted the explanation with nods.

"We're happy to meet with law enforcement or their representatives whenever necessary to help catch this person," Marta told them. Her face took on a sour expression. "We could have been killed. And now, the same thing has happened to two other homes in the neighborhood."

"Are you planning to rebuild?" Courtney asked.

Willy let out a shallow sigh. "We haven't made that decision yet. We'll meet with the insurance company to go over the figures. Marta and I aren't sure if we want to stay in the house or not. I don't know if we'd always feel unsafe."

"We raised our three children in that house," Marta chimed in. "We loved it, but now, we aren't sure what to do. We might just knock the place down and sell the lot." A few tears gathered in the woman's eyes. "We lost so much in the fire ... old photographs, some heirloom furniture handed down to us by our parents, two valuable paintings. I guess we'll take our memories with us wherever we go, but the whole thing has been heartbreaking."

Willy straightened his shoulders and kept a stoic

look on his face. "Our kids are grown and living outside of Boston, but they're very upset at the loss of the family home."

Angie nodded.

"It's a terrible loss for your family," Courtney empathized.

"Can you run us through the evening of the fire?" Angie asked. "To give us a sense of what happened and when it happened."

Marta took a quick sip of her coffee. "It was a normal evening. Willy and I read in the living room until it was time for bed. We each had a small cup of tea and then retired to our room."

"We both dozed off quickly. We'd been out most of the day on a hike and we were worn out," Willy said.

"What time did you go to bed?" Angie asked.

"It was right around 11pm," Marta said.

"Did you see or hear anything out of the normal before you went to your room?" Angie questioned.

"It was a chilly night," Willy said. "We had the windows closed. We didn't notice anything at all."

"What happened next?" Courtney asked.

Marta swallowed hard. "The fire alarm went off. It scared the heck out of me. Willy and I woke at the same time. I was disoriented for a few moments."

"The room was full of smoke." Perspiration showed on Willy's forehead and his face flushed from reliving the event.

"Our bedroom door was open. Red light flickered on the wall." Marta's breathing rate had increased.

"The fire. It was reflecting on the bedroom wall from out in the hall." Willy pushed back a little from the table. "When something like that happens ... when some unexpected emergency wakes you from sleep, it takes the mind a few minutes to process the whole thing."

"I jumped out of bed," Marta said. "I screamed at Willy. I told him it was fire. I told him to get up, get out of bed."

"I scrambled to my feet. We were both coughing. The smoke inhibited my ability to think clearly. I just stood there. Marta grabbed my hand and pulled me to the window."

"I was afraid to open it." Marta wrung her hands. "I was afraid the draft from an open window would make the fire spread into our bedroom so I pulled Willy into the master bathroom and slammed the door. I ran to the window and opened it."

"There was a small stool in our bathroom for our grandson when he comes to visit. He stands on it to use the sink. Marta pushed the stool to the window, told me to step onto it and go out the window. My head was clearing slightly from the fresh air coming in through the open window. I made her go first."

"I scrambled out and yelled for Willy to get out of there."

"I climbed out right after Marta did." Willy ran his palm over his forehead. "We held hands and ran into the yard."

"When we turned around," Marta said. "The flames were shooting out of the bathroom window. The one we'd just escaped through. If we were a minute later, we wouldn't have been able to get out."

"We'd be dead," Willy added solemnly.

The four people sat quietly for several moments.

"Thankfully, you made it out," Angie said with a nod. "I'm very sorry this happened to you."

"We had a somewhat similar experience." Courtney shared about the carriage house fire and their own escape from the flames. "When disaster strikes, it makes you appreciate every day, because, really, who knows what tomorrow can bring."

"That is so true," Marta said. "I remember now reading in the news about the fire you had here. I didn't connect it with you. Did it happen about a year and a half ago?"

"That's right," Angie said and then directed the conversation back to the event at the Bensons' house. "When you were out in the yard that night, did you notice anything? Maybe someone hurrying away?"

"We didn't see anything," Willy said. "We were in shock. I don't think we would have seen anything even if someone *was* there."

"What did you do after getting safely out of the house?" Courtney asked the couple.

"The next door neighbor, Ronny Sand, came running over to us." Marta kept her hands clutched together in her lap. "I don't know what he said to us. He was kind. He led us away to his house."

"Ronny had called the fire department," Willy said. "He woke to the fire. He told us he noticed a strange red flashing. Ronny sleeps with his window open. He heard the crackling sounds, took a look outside, called the emergency number, and then ran over to our house to be sure we had gotten out."

"Did Ronny mention seeing anything unusual when he looked outside or when he was going to check on you?" Angie asked.

"We never asked him and he didn't offer any information like that," Willy said.

"Have you talked with any of your other neighbors?" Courtney asked.

"Sure. Nobody saw anything weird. People came out of their homes when they heard the commotion ... the fire trucks, the police sirens. We talked with some of the neighbors right then, but no one mentioned seeing anything unusual. If somebody did see something, they haven't shared it with us."

Marta said, "At the time, we didn't know it was arson. We thought it was an electrical thing that started the fire or maybe a gas leak that ignited somehow. The last thing we would have thought of was arson."

"We almost passed out when the police told us it was a case of arson," Willy said. "My head was swimming. Did someone try to kill us? Who would want us dead? Did we know the person who set the fire? Why would someone do this to us?"

"Did you come up with any answers to those questions?" Angie asked.

"We thought long and hard about it," Marta said. "We talked it over with our kids. Let me tell you, it is a strange and unsettling feeling to think someone is so filled with rage towards you that they would try to end your life."

"We couldn't come up with any reason at all for

someone to set the fire." Willy shook his head. "We couldn't think of a single person who would want to kill us."

"Do the police think it was random?" Courtney questioned.

"They didn't think it was random at first," Marta said. "But after the second fire in the neighborhood, I think they considered that the fires had been set randomly."

"And now, with a third incident, who knows what the police are thinking," Willy said. "Our neighborhood is quiet, it's tree-lined, there's space between the properties, plenty of space to provide cover for someone to sneak up and set a fire."

Marta's face looked angry. "Maybe some firebug drove around looking for the perfect place to terrorize people, and ended up choosing our neighborhood. Lucky us."

Courtney asked, "Is there anyone in the neighborhood who acts sort of odd? Someone who is especially unfriendly or antisocial? Someone who might stand out as a little peculiar?"

Marta and Willy looked at each other and then shrugged.

"We don't know everyone in the neighborhood," Marta said. "We recognize most of the residents though. The people on our street are all pleasant. No one seems odd."

"No one in the neighborhood would do such a terrible thing," Willy said.

Angie wasn't so sure. "Has anyone in the neighborhood ever been arrested for any reason?"

Marta's eyes went wide. "I don't think so."

"Are any of the homes rented out?" Courtney questioned.

"One is," Willy told them. "Wait, two of the houses are rented out. I've talked to the people who are renting. Two young families. They seem quite nice." Willy leaned forward with an earnest expression. "Why on earth would anyone be driven to do such a thing? What is wrong with someone who has the desire to set fire to someone's home?"

Angie wished she had an answer for those questions.

5

After Angie closed the bake shop for the day, she showered and changed, and worked in the kitchen with Mr. Finch making spanakopita and prepping the chicken souvlaki. Now she was mixing together the ingredients for tzatziki sauce while Finch placed the dinner items in the refrigerator. It was game night at the Victorian and family and friends would gather to enjoy dinner prior to playing cards, board games, or charades.

Angie had been telling Mr. Finch about the interview with Marta and Willy Benson.

"Those poor people. Losing their home of more than thirty years." Finch shook his head as Euclid let out a hiss from where he had perched on top of the

41

fridge with Circe. "But thankfully, they escaped and survived. Unfortunately, they didn't have much to say about the possible identity of the arsonist."

"I wonder if the arsonist lives in the Benson's neighborhood." Angie used a wire whisk to mix together the lemon juice, yogurt, dill, and garlic before adding the chopped and strained cucumber. "The couple couldn't think of anyone who might seem troubled or a little off."

Finch said, "Oftentimes, a criminal is able to hide his deceit from others. We know this all too well from the cases we've been involved with."

"Well, tomorrow in the late afternoon, Jenna and I will be interviewing the second arson victim, Bill Bennington. He's staying at the resort for a while," Angie said. "Come along with us, if you have the time."

"I'm opening the candy shop tomorrow so I will be available in the afternoon to accompany you," Finch said.

"Good. It's always helpful to have you along," Angie said.

Wearing a blue dress, heels, and a light coat, Ellie bustled in through the back door carrying two bags of groceries. "I picked up some fruit and some ingredients to make some honey cookies. I was going to make baklava, but I didn't make it home early enough."

"You look nice," Angie noticed how her sister was dressed.

"I went to the town hall to drop off my application for the finance board position." Ellie's lips were turned down and her eyes were narrowed.

"Is something wrong, Miss Ellie?" Finch asked.

The tall blonde was about to dismiss the question, but she changed her mind. "You know what I heard when I was at the town hall? I was submitting the paperwork when two of the finance board members walked past and I heard them whisper when they moved down the hallway."

Angie dried her hands on a dishtowel and gave her sister a serious look. "What did you hear?"

Ellie's jaw set. "One of them said to the other, 'she's too pretty to be taken seriously for the position'."

Angie's eyes flashed. "You're kidding me. Who said that?"

"It was either Peter Murray or Lou Welt. I can't be sure which one it was."

"What did the other man say to that comment?"

"Nothing. He grunted." Ellie removed her coat and hung it on a hook in the entryway."

"You should report them," Angie's voice was louder than usual.

"I really can't do that." Ellie started to remove the items from the shopping bag. "Nobody heard them. They'd deny it."

"But aren't they going to be the ones who interview you for the position?"

"Yes, and one other member of the board, Allison Mets."

"Should you tell Allison what you heard the men say about you?" Angie asked.

"No. I'm going to get that position by being the best-prepared and most knowledgeable candidate." Ellie looked her sister in the eye and gave her a sly smile. "And whether I'm too pretty or not is not going to matter after I blow all the other candidates out of the water."

Mr. Finch applauded.

Ellie laughed. "Of course, I'm all talk. I'm a nervous wreck about it, but I'm working with Jack to practice for the interview and I'm learning everything I can about the board and their responsibilities and the needs of the town. I won't go down without a fight."

Angie beamed at her sister with pride. "I would expect nothing less."

Jenna and Courtney walked into the kitchen from the hall.

"What's cookin'?" Courtney asked. "It smells delicious in here."

"You didn't try it on yet, did you?" Jenna asked Angie.

Angie shook her head. "Of course not. I waited for all of you."

"Good. Shall we?" Jenna smiled. "I can't wait to see how it fits."

The four sisters, two cats, and Mr. Finch climbed the wide staircase to Ellie's suite of rooms where she and Angie went into the bedroom while the others took seats in the front sitting room to wait.

The rectangular box rested on Ellie's bed. The cover had been removed and the bodice of the wedding dress that had belonged to their mother was visible.

"It's so pretty," Ellie said admiring the beadwork. "Nana was quite the seamstress."

Angie smiled. "You got your talent from her."

"Ready? Let's lift it out."

Angie and Ellie put their hands gently under the white material and brought the dress out of the box. The tulle and lace unfolded and the exquisite gown's fabric cascaded down to the floor.

Ellie almost gasped. "Look at how well-preserved it is. It looks brand new."

"Wow," was all Angie could manage.

Sliding the zipper down the back, Ellie held it out for her sister to slip into it. "Let's see how it fits."

Closing the tiny clasp at the back of the neck, Ellie stepped back as Angie turned to her. The tiny crystals and pearls shimmered in the light. The top of the dress perfectly accentuated Angie's figure before the pearly fabric flared out and, with a swish, fell softly around her feet.

"Gosh," Ellie whispered. "It looks like it was made for you."

Angie caught her reflection in the full-length mirror and her jaw almost dropped. Her hand moved to the lace edge below her collarbone and her finger traced the line of the v-neck.

"It's perfect, Angie," Ellie said.

Angie brushed at her eyes and took a deep breath.

"What's going on in there?" Courtney called from the sitting room. "Come out and let us see."

Ellie opened the bedroom door and Angie walked slowly into the room where the others were waiting.

"Whoa," Courtney nearly whooped.

A broad smile crossed over Jenna's face. "You look amazing."

Euclid and Circe jumped down off the small sofa and trilled.

Angie looked over at Mr. Finch just as tears spilled over his lids and slipped down his cheeks. "You look like a princess," the man blubbered.

Everyone chuckled at Finch's display of emotion.

"Wait until the wedding day," Courtney kidded. "Mr. Finch will need a few cases of tissues."

Jenna handed the man a soft facecloth she took from the shelf in Ellie's bathroom and gave him a hug. "You are a sweetheart, Mr. Finch."

"Where is everyone?" Josh's voice was heard out in the hall.

Jenna rushed to the door and slammed it. "You can't come in here. Angie's trying on a dress."

"It's okay," Angie said. "He can come in."

"Oh, no, he can't." Ellie ordered. "Call me old-fashioned, but he will not see your wedding dress until you're walking down the aisle."

Angie said with a grin, "You *are* old-fashioned."

"I know that. Tomorrow, you can try it on again. I want to take it in slightly right here." Ellie pointed to the waist. "And once you get your shoes, I'll manage the hem. Now, let's get you out of it. We need to finish preparing the meal before everyone arrives for game night."

Ellie herded her sister back into the bedroom. "And Mr. Finch is right. You do look like a princess ... the most beautiful princess ever."

THE MEDITERRANEAN MEAL was a huge success with the guests.

"That was scrumptious," Betty Hayes, Mr. Finch's girlfriend, said. "I haven't had kebobs and spanakopita for ages."

"Compliments to the chefs." Chief Martin rubbed his stomach.

Jenna's husband, Tom, came around the table with two different bottles of wine to fill everyone's glasses.

"Rufus and I brought a dessert to contribute to the meal." Jack adjusted his bow tie. "We made it ourselves."

"It took most of the day," Rufus laughed. "We spent six hours on it. We kept messing up."

"It was a difficult dish to prepare?" Finch asked.

"Well, it was for us." Rufus Fudge, an Englishman, was a newly-minted attorney who worked in Jack's law office. He was also Courtney's boyfriend.

Jack got up to help Ellie and Courtney clear the table and Rufus went to the kitchen to make tea and coffee.

Tom stifled a yawn. "I'm beat. We've been working all-out to finish a construction project on deadline. My contribution to the evening will have to be my pleasant company because I'm too tired to get out of this chair and help."

"Too tired for a game of cards?" Finch asked the man.

Tom gave Finch a mock-evil look. "Never too tired to whoop you at cards."

Rufus carried in a tray with tea and coffee pots and cream and sugar. "If anyone is going to be doing any whooping, it's going to be me."

"Bring it on," Mr. Finch dared.

Betty rolled her eyes. "Such cutthroat behavior over a simple game of cards."

Chief Martin's wife, Lucille, said, "It must be something left over from the days of early man."

"That could be," Courtney said as she rolled up her sleeves. "But tonight, the men are making room at the table for me. I'm challenging them at their own game."

Circe trilled from where she sat on top of the China cabinet.

"Let the card-sharks do their trash-talking," Angie said. "Anyone want to join me in playing a word game?"

Three people raised their hands and the other four at the table decided on a different board game.

After desserts were served and much praise was heaped on Rufus and Jack for their homemade baklava, the group divided up to play their games. The Scrabble players remained at the dining room table, the card players went to sit at the square card table set up by the fire, and the other board game group settled at the second card table in the living room.

Ellie put on some music and for thirty minutes, the rooms filled with chatter and laughter and, from one table in particular, a bit more trash-talking could be heard.

Chief Martin formed a high-value word and leaned over to Angie. "It's great to have a night off and get away from troubles."

"You can say that again." Angie nodded and took her turn making a word on the board.

The chief's phone buzzed and with a sigh, he took it from his pocket and read the message.

Angie glanced at him and when she saw his expression, she said, "Oh, no."

Chief Martin reluctantly announced, "There's another fire," and suddenly, the game-players all went silent.

6

So as not to ruin game night at the Victorian, only Angie and Jenna accompanied Chief Martin to Silver Cove.

"This time it's different," the chief told them as they rode in the squad car. "This time it's not a residential fire. It's a business."

"Maybe it's not the arsonist," Jenna said with a tinge of hope. "Maybe this one happened due to faulty wiring or something. Is it a restaurant?"

"It's an accountant's office in the center of Silver Cove," the chief informed them. "It seems the place was closed for the day. No one was inside."

"Do you think it might not be related to the other fires?" Angie asked.

The chief frowned. "I think it *is* related to the

others, but I hope an investigation proves me wrong."

"Is it unusual for an arsonist to choose a different kind of target?" Angie asked. "Do most firebugs usually hit the same kind of building or structure?"

"There isn't really a definitive pattern for the choosing of a site."

"Is there a profile for an arsonist?" Angie asked. "Or is every one of them different?"

"There is a profile," the chief said. "But it has to be taken with a grain of salt because the information was gathered from wildfire arsonists. Not many arsonists get arrested and then there are the different motives for setting fires which can change the profile of the people who do it." Chief Martin let out a sigh. "That said, I can tell you some character-istics of a fire setter."

"Let me guess," Jenna said while watching the dark trees flash by the car window. "Antisocial behavior."

"That's one of them," the chief said.

"What else should we be looking out for?" Angie asked.

"Poor academic performance. Usually the person is intelligent, but works in low-paying jobs that don't suit the person's abilities."

"Interesting," Angie said. "The person is smart, but he doesn't meet his potential."

"The person often has a fascination with fire-fighters or the fire service. If he got married, he is often divorced. If he never married, he is often living at home with his parents. Poor social skills, so no friends or his relationships are unstable or of low quality."

"Anything else?" Jenna asked.

"It is usually a white male under the age of thirty. It's not uncommon for the person to have trouble with alcohol or drugs."

"Does an arsonist come from a broken home?" Angie questioned.

"Sometimes. One or both parents may be missing from the household or there is a poor relationship with parents. The mother may be overbearing, the father may be indifferent or cold," the chief reported as he turned the car onto the main street of Silver Cove.

They didn't get very far before the flashing lights of emergency vehicles could be seen in the distance. The chief pulled the car to the side of the road. "We'll have to walk the last few blocks. We won't be allowed to get any closer with the car."

Jenna and Angie emerged from the vehicle and

stood on the dark sidewalk watching some of the orange flames shooting out of the second floor windows. Smoke tainted the air and caused Jenna to cough. They got closer to the hubbub by way of the chief showing his identification and being waved along by security personnel.

"It's gone up to the second floor," Angie observed.

"Everyone got out safely," the chief said after having a few words with a colleague. "No one is inside. I'm going to speak with some of the officers. I'll be back in a bit."

A shudder ran over Angie's skin as she imagined being trapped inside the burning building and a wave of gratitude washed over her after hearing the place had been unoccupied when the blaze started. "It's lucky no one is in there."

Jenna moved closer to her sister. "Does it seem odd that the person would choose to set a fire in a business rather than a home? He's changing his way of operating."

"It probably makes sense though." Angie kept her eyes on the emergency personnel. "The Park River neighborhood has been hit three times. The arsonist might have assumed there were too many people on the lookout for trouble. He needed a new area. A place no one expected."

"He's probably getting a thrill out of everyone's surprise at the new location," Jenna said with an angry tone as she turned her gaze on the people gathered on the sidewalks to watch the firefighters battling the blaze. "Do you think he's here?"

"The arsonist?" Angie's eyes were wide.

"Do you think he's pretending to be a bystander so he can get an eyeful of what he's done?" Jenna asked. "So he can get high on the excitement?"

"The chief told us the arsonist might have an obsession with fire personnel," Angie scanned the crowd. "If he *is* here, he could watch the firefighters work and he can get a thrill from all the chaos he's created."

"Let's wander around," Jenna suggested. "Let's walk through the crowd, see if anyone stands out as being too excited by the commotion."

The sisters wandered past the groups of people gathered here and there on Main Street watching as the fire was subdued.

Three young men of college age stood outside of a pub restaurant chuckling and making stupid jokes and comments about what was going on. Angie and Jenna stopped to listen and observe them, being careful to make note of the men's appearances, voices, and behavior.

When they'd watched the threesome for about five minutes, they decided to move along to see as many people as possible.

"Those guys were jerks, but I don't know if that makes them arsonists," Angie said.

"Don't firebugs usually work alone?" Jenna asked.

"I think that's right. So maybe one of them set it and then joined his friends?"

"Possibly," Jenna said with hesitation. "I don't know why, but I don't think any of them did it."

"Let's keep looking," Angie led the way to another group of observers where she lingered at the edge of the gathering watching each person stare at the fire.

A blond teenager wearing jeans and a t-shirt kept his face turned to the emergency workers, a couple stared at the trucks and hoses and personnel rushing back and forth, a middle-aged man stood slightly off to the side his wide eyes pinned on the fire, his cheeks flushed red.

"A lot of people look excited by the fire," Jenna whispered.

"Do you feel something from any of them?" Angie asked.

Jenna paused before responding. "I don't think so. If the arsonist was near, wouldn't we feel something stronger than suspicion?"

"I don't know what to expect." Angie gave a shrug and they started away along the sidewalk to move to the next group.

"How can we find this guy?" Jenna asked. "Has anyone actually seen him? Unless he makes a mistake, how can we zero in on him? He hides among all of us, darting in to set a fire, and then darting away."

"He'll make a mistake." Angie's jaw set and she shoved her hands into her jacket pockets. "We just have to wait for it."

"I hope he messes up soon because if this goes on too long, someone is going to get hurt." Jenna held her sister's eyes. "Or worse."

The main street of Silver Cove consisted of restaurants and a few pubs next to shops and stores. This particular end of the street had more businesses ... a lawyer's office, a hair stylist, a small specialty market, a dentist, a dog groomer, and the accountant's suite on the first floor of the burning three-story building.

"What's on the second and third floor of that building?" Angie asked, her eyes narrowed trying to find a sign that indicated what was inside the structure.

"I don't know." Jenna moved a few yards to the right to talk to a couple of gawkers. "Do you know what businesses are in the building?"

The young woman said, "There's an accountant on the first floor. I think there's a doctor's office and a physical therapist upstairs."

The young woman's companion said, "The third floor was going to be four apartments. Construction was going on up there. I wonder if the renovations caused the fire."

Jenna went back to Angie to tell her what she heard.

"Chief Martin will tell us if the construction work was the cause of the fire," Angie said. "But I think it was set."

"I agree." Jenna pushed her long brown hair over her shoulder. "There's something on the air ... something besides smoke."

The words Angie was going to say in reply caught in her throat as a cold breeze blew over the sidewalks and made her shiver. Quickly turning around, she stared at some people standing a half-block away. Something picked at her, and she strode off to get closer to the group. Jenna hurried to catch up to her.

"What is it?"

"I don't know. I feel strange." Angie's eyes flashed around unsure of what she was looking for.

"Do you think the person responsible for the fire is around here?" Jenna asked, nervousness running through her body.

Someone caught Angie's attention as he moved away from the crowd and walked with purpose to a side street that ran off of Main.

Angie quickened her pace. She hadn't seen his face.

The man was of average height and had a slim build. His hair was dark. From the back, he looked to be in his twenties or thirties. He wore a long-sleeved collared shirt with dress slacks giving the impression he was a businessman or a professional of some sort.

When the sisters made the corner, the man wasn't on the sidewalk or in the street. Other people walked past, but he wasn't among them.

"Where did he go?" Angie asked with frustration in her voice.

The two young women stood still and turned in

circles under a streetlight trying to find the man, but they couldn't locate him.

"How could he just disappear?" Jenna asked. "Did he drive off in a car?"

Angie blew out a breath. "Did we just lose the arsonist? Did he slip through our fingers? Was that him?"

A cold shiver ran down Angie's back like an icy hand tracing along her spine.

ngie's bake shop buzzed with the early morning activity as customers came and went with drinks and sweets, and others sat at the café tables chatting with friends or colleagues.

Louisa, Angie's friend and employee, carried a new tray of cinnamon rolls, handmade donuts and bagels, buttery scones, flaky croissants, and squares of coffee cakes to the glass case. "Everything's selling so fast this morning. I hope we don't run out."

"We might need to increase our inventory to meet the demand," Angie said as she made a latte for a customer. "I'll have to go over the numbers to be sure the need is consistent."

The ends of Louisa's ebony hair were dyed a

lovely shade of blue and she had it piled on top of her head in a loose, pretty bun. "At least it's a good problem to have," the young woman smiled.

When the door to the shop opened, Angie saw the delighted look on Louisa's face and she knew who must have entered the room.

Lance McCullough, a skilled carpenter who worked on one of Tom's construction and renovation crews, beamed at Louisa as he approached the counter and took one of the empty stools. He and Louisa had been dating and the two were smitten with each other. "Morning," he said to both women.

Louisa cheeks flushed pink as she leaned across the counter and gave Lance a quick kiss.

"I hear you and your sisters are helping out the police with the Silver Cove arson cases," Lance said to Angie. The young man had an apartment in Silver Cove close to Main Street.

"We are," Angie nodded. "You didn't happen to see anything the other night, did you?"

"Sorry. I was here in town with Louisa." Lance sipped from the coffee mug his girlfriend had brought over. "It scared me, I'm not ashamed to say. That building going up in flames. It's only two blocks from where I live. That arsonist has got me spooked."

"I think a lot of people feel the same way," Angie told him. "I know I would if I lived in Silver Cove."

"Are the police close to catching the guy?" Lance asked.

The look on Angie's face told the whole story.

"Too bad. I guess I was too hopeful about it getting solved quick," Lance said.

"You know you can stay with me any time you don't feel comfortable at your place," Louisa said with a little smile.

"I appreciate it." Lance returned the grin. "I wish there was something I could do to help find the person."

Angie said, "Keep your eyes open. Be watchful. If you see anything suspicious, call the police, or take down a license plate. And it wouldn't hurt if you kept a light on in your apartment at night. From what I understand, an arsonist will often move on if they think someone is awake in the home or building he's targeting. He won't take a chance of being seen."

Lance said, "Good advice. I'll do that. Thanks, Angie."

Another good-looking man entered the bake shop and this time, Angie was the one who beamed at the person.

Josh Williams took a seat next to Lance and

smiled at his fiancée. "I'm heading up to Salem for a business meeting so I stopped to pick up a coffee to take on the drive."

Josh and Lance talked while Louisa and Angie waited on customers, and when there was a break in the action, they joined the men in conversation.

"I was thinking," Angie looked at Josh. "I'd really like to make our wedding cake."

Josh tilted his head slightly. "Well, I wouldn't say no to my favorite baker making our cake, but would it be too much? You'll be getting ready, there will be a lot going on ... hair, makeup, pictures being taken. You don't want to be stressed by having to manage the cake, too."

"The cake will be finished the night before. I'll only have to make a few finishing touches after it arrives at the resort."

"That would be great then. I already know the flavor I'd like."

The corners of Angie's mouth turned up. "Let me guess. Could it be carrot cake?"

"You know me too well."

"I was thinking of doing different flavors for each of the cake layers," Angie said. "Of course, the biggest layer will be carrot cake."

"As long as I get my favorite flavor, you can

choose all of the others." Josh smiled as he took a bite of his chocolate croissant.

"It's a deal," Angie agreed.

When Louisa walked Lance to the door, Angie lowered her voice when she said to Josh, "Jenna, Mr. Finch, and I are interviewing one of the guests at the resort later this afternoon."

"The man who lost his home to the arsonist?" Josh asked.

"Yes, Bill Bennington. Have you met him?"

"When he first came to the resort, I spoke with him. He was justifiably upset. I gave him his first two nights in his suite for free. I don't know how long he plans to stay. Initially, he mentioned two weeks, but one of the desk clerks told me Mr. Bennington had inquired about staying longer."

"Is he working in the area?" Angie asked. "Maybe he isn't able to go too far from Sweet Cove."

"I didn't ask what he did for work. I don't know if his home is salvageable or if it's a lost cause. The man doesn't like questions about the fire."

Angie raised an eyebrow. "Then he won't like it when we show up to ask him about the fire. I wonder if this interview isn't going to go well."

"You and Jenna can put the Roseland charm on him," Josh said. "And Mr. Finch always wins people over with his warm and friendly manner." Looking up at the wall clock, Josh said, "I need to get going or I'm going to be late for the meeting. Good luck this afternoon." He squeezed Angie's hand. "We need to decide about the furniture for the new apartment. Maybe tonight we can go over everything."

Angie and Josh had to choose the furnishings for the apartment that had just been built for them on the third floor of the Victorian.

"Only a few weeks until the wedding," Josh grinned and then kidded, "And then I get to realize my dream of living in a Victorian mansion."

Angie bopped him on the arm and narrowed her eyes. "What about your dream of living with me?"

"Oh, right. That's what I meant," Josh teased and got up fast from his stool to avoid another bop from his fiancée.

"See you tonight," Angie waved as she went to wait on a customer.

ANGIE, Jenna, and Mr. Finch sat in the sitting room of Bill Bennington's suite of rooms in the Sweet Cove Resort. The man, in his early sixties, had a full head of gray hair and intense blue eyes. He was over six feet tall and had the slim body of a runner.

The Roseland sisters and Finch offered the man condolences on the loss of his house.

"Will you be able to have the house repaired?" Finch asked. "Will you return to live in it?"

"I just don't know. I feel violated. I feel my safety and sense of security has been stolen from me," Bennington said as he rubbed his forehead. "I don't know if I want to return to the place or not."

"Other people affected by the fire have said the same thing," Angie told the man.

"The Bensons? I know them. We don't socialize or anything, but I run into them frequently on the trails in the park that runs along the ocean. I spoke with them briefly. They told me they weren't sure if they'll move to another town or will move back into their house once it's been repaired."

"It might be too soon to make that decision," Jenna said. "It will take time to process the event ... and your feelings about it."

"What do you do for work?" Finch asked Bennington hoping to build a rapport with him.

Bennington sighed. "I'm a psychiatrist. I work in the hospital on the edge of Silver Cove. I have an office there as well."

"Do you have family or friends in the area?" Angie asked.

"Family is gone, but I have quite a few friends living in the area towns. I was offered accommodations with several people, but I didn't take them up on it. I like being able to retreat to my own rooms to read or research and besides, I didn't want to inconvenience them. I don't know how long it will take to renovate and repair my home."

"Will you stay here at the resort until then?" Jenna asked.

"If they have the availability," Bennington said. "It's very pleasant here, the rooms, the grounds. Very nice. It takes my mind off the troubles."

"Would you mind telling us about the night of the fire?" Angie asked.

"I *would* mind. I can't stand reliving and retelling about that awful night." Bennington shook his head slowly from side to side and let out a long sigh. "But if I must, I must. I understand you are working with the police to apprehend the arsonist so I will repeat my tale once again."

Angie expressed her appreciation for Bennington's cooperation.

"It was late, about midnight. I was reading in the den at the back of the house. I like to have a window open. It was a pleasant evening, but the night had turned cool. I hadn't shut the window yet."

"Did you hear anything?" Finch sat near the edge of his seat holding the top of his cane in his hands.

"An owl hooted a few times and I heard sort of a rustling sound. I think it was a breeze in the trees."

"What did it sound like?" Angie asked. "Can you be more specific about what you heard?"

"Well, let me think." Bennington's face screwed up in thought. "It was like leaves blowing gently over a sidewalk, or like leaves moving in the trees from a breeze."

"But the leaves aren't fully out yet," Jenna explained. "Mostly, there are only buds on the branches."

"Hmm." Bennington placed his hands together, his index fingers pointing towards the ceiling. "You're right. Then what could have been the source of what I heard?"

"Had you heard the noise before that night?" Mr. Finch asked.

Bennington's lips almost formed a pout. "Maybe not. I read in the den almost every night. I don't believe I heard the noise on previous evenings."

"Maybe it was someone walking past your window?" Jenna asked.

"That could be it. There are still some leaves left-over from the fall in the backyard," Bennington said. "Someone may have been walking through them."

Angie wanted to hear about the man's experience once the fire started. "Had the fire started by then?"

Bennington nodded. "I wanted to finish the chapter I was reading, but then I heard a crackling sound. I got up to go and investigate when I smelled the smoke, I stopped in my tracks."

"Did the fire alarm go off?" Jenna asked.

"It did almost immediately after I smelled smoke."

"What happened then?" Angie questioned.

"I froze. Things didn't seem real. A fire in my home? It couldn't be possible."

Finch asked the man, "Was the door to the den open?"

"It was. The smoke came heavy then. It all happened so fast. I could see the red flashes against the hallway wall."

"What did you do?"

"I moved towards the hall, but I could feel the heat right away so I grabbed my phone from the side table and rushed to the window. I pushed up the window and squeezed through it and landed on my shoulder on the ground. I got up and stumbled into the rear yard. I'll never forget the sight. Flames rising from the house. I called 911 for the firefighters. I was numb. I don't even remember what happened next."

"Did you notice anyone lurking? Anyone hurrying away?" Angie asked.

"Nothing. No one." Bennington blinked a few times. "My neighbor ran over. He stayed with me until help arrived."

"Mr. Bennington, I have hard questions to ask, questions many people don't like to hear," Angie told him.

"It's okay. You can ask what you need to." The man's voice was even.

"Do you have any enemies?"

Bennington didn't hesitate. "Oh, well, sure, I do."

8

With cups of tea, Angie, Jenna, and Finch gathered at the kitchen island with Courtney and Ellie to tell about the interview with Bill Bennington. The cats were in position on top of the refrigerator listening to the chatter.

Jenna said, "And when Angie asked if Mr. Bennington had any enemies, he told us he sure did. Like it wasn't anything unusual to have people who hate you."

"People actually hate him?" Courtney frowned as she took a chocolate ding dong from the platter on the counter.

"He claimed that it is impossible to go through

life without making enemies." Finch stirred a little sugar into his hot tea.

"Is that true, Mr. Finch?" Courtney handed the man one of the ding dongs. "You've lived a long time and no one hates you."

"I suppose for some people it is true." Finch dabbed a bit of the sugary filling from his lip. "For example, my brother, Thaddeus. A mean and nasty man. But I like to think you get what you give in life so, yes, it *is* possible to go through life without making an enemy."

Courtney placed another ding dong on Finch's dessert plate. "Do you mind if I ask how old you are, Mr. Finch?"

Ellie scolded her younger sister. "That isn't polite."

"Why isn't it though? Mr. Finch knows how old all of us are. He's part of our family. It's okay to ask."

"I'd rather not say, Miss Courtney. You might be surprised by my answer."

"Really?" Courtney asked with a grin. "What? Are you really around twenty-five, or something?"

"Or something." Finch returned the young woman's grin.

The cats trilled from their high perch.

"I'll get it out of you someday." Courtney winked.

"Of that, I am quite sure." Finch took another sip from his teacup. "Until that day, I will keep my number of years on this planet a secret."

"Did Mr. Bennington tell you who his enemies are?" Ellie questioned.

"It's Dr. Bennington. He's a psychiatrist," Angie said. "He was vague. A couple of colleagues who are jealous of his publications. Some patients who didn't think he did enough for them. A neighbor because they argued over a property boundary."

"Did the property dispute take place at the house he lives in now?" Ellie asked.

"No, it was years ago," Jenna said.

"Did you ask if any of the people who are not fond of him could be an arsonist?" Courtney asked.

"We did ask," Finch said. "He wasn't sure."

"This guy sounds like a nut." Ellie crossed her arms over her chest. "How can he be a psychiatrist? How can he be so odd and be of any help to others?"

"Maybe he's too practical or pragmatic or pessimistic," Angie said. "Maybe he doesn't see the world the way we do."

"I think that's plain." Courtney went to the fridge to get a glass of milk. "Has Bennington ever been married?"

"He was married for two years," Angie said. "The marriage ended in divorce."

"Any kids?"

"No, none."

"I guess that's a good thing." Courtney downed a third of the milk in her glass. "That's one of the characteristics of an arsonist. Trouble with relationships. Could Bennington be our man?"

"He doesn't fit the age profile," Finch offered.

"He also doesn't fit the part about being an academic underachiever," Angie pointed out.

"Okay, that's true. Then I guess he's off the list of possible firebugs," Courtney said.

Ellie took a seat at the counter next to Jenna. "Do some arsonists destroy their own property? Do they set fire to their own homes?"

"That's a good question." Angie took a bowl of fruit salad out of the refrigerator and placed it on the island with some small bowls and spoons. "I wouldn't be surprised if an arsonist set his own house on fire to divert attention away from himself. But we need to ask Chief Martin if we should consider a victim as a possible suspect."

Courtney scooped some fruit into a bowl and began to eat. "If the chief says yes to that question, then I'm putting Bill Bennington back on the suspect list despite his age and professional status. I think he should be spoken to again. And what was that rustling noise he says he heard? From what you tell us, he didn't explain it very well."

"Bennington will be staying at the resort for the foreseeable future so we can arrange to speak to him again if we think it's warranted," Angie said.

"Who's next up to interview?" Ellie arranged some cookies on a blue and white platter for the B and B guests.

Angie said, "Chief Martin arranged a time to meet with the young couple whose house was targeted by the arsonist. Randi and Jon Willoughby. They're in their late twenties. The meeting is set for tomorrow afternoon. Any volunteers?"

"I'll go with you if Mr. Finch will handle the candy store," Courtney offered.

"I'd be glad to," Finch nodded.

"I really can't get away," Ellie said. "I need to do more research for my interview for the finance board seat and I'm meeting with some of the guests to go over what they should see while they're here on the North Shore."

"Can you two handle it?" Jenna asked. "I need to get some jewelry orders out."

"We'll manage it, right, sis?" Courtney gave

Angie a little bump with her elbow. "Maybe we'll learn something important."

RANDI AND JON WILLOUGHBY sat across from Courtney and Angie on the sofa in the living room of their friend's house.

The Willoughbys were in their late twenties and both looked athletic and fit. Randi had long, wavy auburn hair and green eyes and Jon was blond with blue eyes.

"I still can't believe our house went up in flames," Randi said with a sad expression. "We loved that house."

"The location was perfect," Jon said. "Hiking trails right near the ocean that we could walk to. A nice neighborhood ... good people around. We looked all over before finding that house. It was perfect for us. It's a ten-minute walk to our office."

"What do you do for work?" Angie asked the couple.

"We buy properties, fix them up, and sell," Jon said. "We keep some of the houses we buy to rent them out. Randi is a licensed Realtor and we're both architects. We have a lot of experience with home improvement."

"Do you plan to return to your own house?" Courtney asked.

Jon nodded. "We're determined to stay. We're talking to the insurance company and we'll see what we can do to fix the place."

"I would think they'll give you what you need to make your house a home again," Angie said.

"We hope so," Randi told the sisters. "We have our fingers crossed. It's our home and we want to go back to it."

"Can you tell us about that night?" Courtney asked with a gentle tone.

"Sure." Randi bit her lower lip. It was clear from the look on her face that it was difficult to talk about. "We had stayed up later than usual. I was doing some bookkeeping and Jon was doing some sketches of a kitchen design. We were working at the kitchen table."

"I had a headache and it started to get worse so I stopped for the night and headed for the bedroom," Jon said.

"I was going to stay up for another thirty minutes," Randi said.

"I took a couple of painkillers and went to bed,"

Jon said. "As soon as I closed my eyes, I started to feel ill. I was afraid I was getting a migraine. Do you get migraines?"

Courtney shook her head.

"I get them, but only rarely," Angie said.

"I get them. Maybe four times a month. I sometimes get the visual aura or sometimes I smell something odd that makes me feel sick. I smelled something that night. I had the window open a few inches to get some fresh air. I thought the odor was just the beginning of the migraine, but later I realized what I was smelling was the alcohol consumed by the arsonist."

"The kitchen is at one end of the house and our bedroom is at the other end down the hall," Randi said. "The fire started in the middle of the house and spread fast. I couldn't get to Jon."

"The bedroom window jammed in position. I couldn't get it to budge. Smoke poured into the room. I was panicking. I tried to find something to bash out the glass, but there wasn't anything that would do the job. I wrapped my arm in towels and was about to try and smash my hand through the glass...." Jon smiled at his wife. "But my hero saved me."

"I ran outside," Randi said. "I ran to the window

of our bedroom. I was terrified because Jon wasn't outside. He was still in the house. We'd been messing around in the yard the other day, playing baseball. We took turns pitching and hitting. I found the bat on the grass and bashed in the window glass. Jon was able to get out through the window."

"Randi stayed calm and level-headed. That's what got me out."

"No, that wasn't what got you out," Randi said with a slight smile. "It was love and devotion, plain and simple. If I couldn't get you out through that window, I would have gone back inside. We're a team. I was not leaving you. It wasn't an option. It just wasn't." A single tear ran down Randi's cheek. Her husband wiped it gently away, wrapped his arm around her, and pulled her close.

Touched by the couple's depth of emotion, Angie had to clear her throat before asking the next question. "In retrospect, did you notice anything that night that now might have seemed unusual?"

Randi and Jon looked at one another.

"I don't think so," Randi said.

Jon shrugged. "I didn't notice anything."

"What about a smell? Or someone you didn't know walking around the neighborhood? Maybe a noise?" Courtney tried to jog the couple's memories.

"We took a walk about an hour before the fire started," Randi said. "We wanted to move a little. We'd been working for hours. We didn't see anyone else walking around."

"I didn't notice any odors except for a heavy smell of alcohol that I assume was from the arsonist standing just outside my window," Jon said. "I didn't hear anything out of the ordinary."

"We did see Officer Pandy drive by," Randi said. "He's with the Silver Cove police. Sometimes the police did rounds, driving through the neighborhood. They started to do that right after the second fire happened."

"They were trying to dissuade the arsonist from striking again." Jon frowned and his voice hardened. "It didn't work."

9

 ngie sat at the kitchen table with Jenna standing behind her plaiting her sister's hair.

Courtney was busy working at the counter making empanadas. "What hairstyle are you doing now?"

"This one is a plaited updo," Jenna said reaching for a bobby pin.

The hairstyles had been going on for about an hour with everyone commenting on what they liked and didn't like about each one.

"My scalp is getting sore," Angie said.

"We have to do this," Jenna told her twin. "We keep putting it off."

"You can't wait until the day of the wedding to make your choice, sis," Courtney said.

Ellie and Mr. Finch were sitting on opposite sides of the kitchen island. Finch was play-acting an interview situation with the young woman to help her prepare for the questioning when she met with the members of the finance board.

Finch said to Angie, "No matter the hairstyle, you will look beautiful. Choose whatever feels best. I've loved them all."

"Mr. Finch, please stay in character," Ellie said to the older man. "Otherwise, I'll lose my train of thought."

"Aren't you ready for that interview yet?" Courtney asked as she used the tines of a fork to press and seal the edges of the empanadas. "You've been practicing for forever. Every question known to man must have been asked of you by now."

"You can never be too prepared." Ellie pushed her long blond hair over her shoulder. "I want to go into that room as confidant as I can be."

"I feel like I could interview for that position," Courtney said. "I've heard every question and answer possible. I can recite them by heart." She asked herself a finance question out loud and then gave the answer. "See? I can do more if you want to hear them."

Angie chuckled.

"Please don't," Ellie said. "I'm getting distracted. Maybe we should move into the sunroom, Mr. Finch."

"Give Mr. Finch a break," Courtney suggested. "Why don't we all have some tea and relax for a few minutes?"

"Good idea." Jenna put the final pin in Angie's hair. "My fingers are seizing up from all this braiding."

"Wow, that's gorgeous," Courtney said eyeing the hairstyle. "Each new style you do is better than the last one. I think this is my favorite."

Euclid and Circe trilled.

Ellie checked out the newest updo. "Beautiful. I love it."

"Stunning," Mr. Finch said. "But that's how you look every day."

Angie thanked the family for their opinions and then went into the bathroom to inspect the hairdo in the mirror. When she returned to the kitchen, she said, "I think this one is the winner."

"Leave it in and show Josh when he gets back," Jenna suggested. "He needs to give his opinion, too."

"Isn't that bad luck to show the fiancé before the wedding?" Ellie poured tea into the mugs for everyone.

"Oh, for Pete's sake," Courtney shook her head. "This is the twenty-first century. Can we move away from the customs of the dark ages?"

"One cannot tempt fate," Ellie said as she delivered the tea.

"Showing someone a hairstyle isn't going to bring misery down on the couple," Courtney said.

Ellie harrumphed.

Jenna sat down and sipped her tea. "Let's move away from speculation about bad luck and talk about the arson cases."

"That *is* talking about bad luck," Ellie protested. "Those poor people who had their houses damaged."

"I've been wondering," Jenna said. "Do you think the arsonist knows his victims?"

Both Circe and Euclid let out simultaneous howls.

"I suppose it's possible," Angie said. "But does that mean the arsonist has a grudge against each victim?"

"I'm more inclined to say the victims are simply convenient for the firebug," Courtney said. "Those houses were secluded enough, but not isolated. I think this guy wants an audience. That's why he moved from setting houses on fire in a quiet neighborhood to hitting a business building on Main Street. Just a bunch of neighbors wasn't enough attention anymore for his work. He needs more people to see his fires. He wants a bigger audience now."

"His obsession with attention will cause him to seek out bigger or more important targets," Finch guessed. "The person's needs are escalating."

"We really need to figure this out soon," Jenna said with worry in her voice. "Do the police have anything new to add to what we know?"

Angie shook her head. "They're running into dead ends."

"What's the next thing we can do to look for answers?" Finch asked.

"I think we should speak with the older couple who live next door to Randi and Jon Willoughby's house," Angie told the family. "When we were there on the night of the fire, they were standing on their front porch. Chief Martin went over to let them know Randi and Jon were okay. I got a strange feeling when I saw the couple. I wonder if they might be able to help us. Maybe they saw or heard something that could point us in an important direction."

"It sure can't hurt to talk with them," Courtney said.

"Chief Martin is in touch with the Silver Cove police?" Finch questioned.

"He is," Angie said. "They're working closely together on this."

"What about that man you saw on the night of the business building fire?" Ellie asked. "You had a feeling of alarm when you saw him."

Angie sighed. "I didn't get a look at his face. Something about him made me feel very odd. I wanted to get a better look at him, but when we turned the corner, he was no where to be seen."

"What did you say he looked like?" Ellie asked.

"Like a bunch of other people," Angie frowned. "Average height, slim, dark hair. He was dressed business casual. Nice slacks, a button-down shirt. He looks like a thousand other men."

"Nothing stood out about him," Jenna added. "Except that he made Angie feel weird."

"I felt a sense of alarm when I spotted him." Angie shook her head. "I don't know why exactly, but there was ... something." Her voice trailed off.

"Are there any surveillance cameras in that area

of Silver Cove?" Finch asked. "Some businesses might have some security cameras in operation. Perhaps, you might see your man on one of the videos?"

"That's a great idea," Courtney said with excitement. "If there are cameras around, Angie might be able to find that guy in the crowd."

"I'll talk to Chief Martin about it," Angie nodded. "It's definitely worth looking into."

"He'll be here in a few minutes," Ellie said absently.

"He's coming over this evening?" Jenna asked. "I didn't know that."

"Neither did I." Angie eyed her blond sister. Ellie sometimes "knew" when someone was coming to the house when the others didn't.

The back door opened and Tom entered the kitchen with a *hello* for everyone. When he spotted Jenna at the table, his eyes lit up and he went over to kiss her. "Chief Martin's outside finishing up a call. He'll be right in."

Angie gave Courtney, Jenna, and Mr. Finch a shrug before turning to Ellie. "Did the chief tell you he was coming over?"

Ellie's face was blank and she blinked fast a couple of times. "I don't know. Maybe."

"Or maybe not." Courtney went to the sink to rinse out her mug.

Euclid swished his huge orange plume of a tail back and forth as he stared down at Ellie with a look of impatience.

The chief knocked and came into the house. "Sorry to bother."

"It's never a bother to have you drop by," Finch smiled at the man. "How about a cup of tea or coffee?"

"Coffee would be great. Thanks," the chief said taking a seat at the table next to Finch. "I was driving by and thought I'd stop. We didn't talk yesterday."

Angie updated the chief on the interview they'd done with Randi and Jon Willoughby. "They're a nice couple. They're determined to rebuild their home and stay in the Park River neighborhood. They won't be driven out by the arsonist."

"Good for them." The chief gratefully accepted the mug of coffee Courtney handed to him. "I'm not sure if I'd do the same or not. No one really knows how they would react to being victimized."

"I don't think I'd stay," Ellie said. "I think I'd be frightened. I don't think I'd ever feel safe in the house again."

"I think I'd want to move," Tom told the group.

"I'd feel worried that Jenna would be at risk if we stayed in a burned up house."

"That's how I'd feel, too." Jenna smiled at her husband. "I'd feel worried *you* would be at risk if we stayed. I'd be afraid to lose you."

"You two can make moon-eyes at each other while the rest of us discuss the case," Courtney said. "Did the Willoughby couple hear or see anything prior to the fire?"

"No," Angie said. "It was a normal evening. They'd been working for hours. Jon headed off to bed, but Randi wanted to keep working for a little while. Jon was trapped in the bedroom when the fire broke out. Randi saved him by breaking in the bedroom window from the outside with a bat."

Jenna shuddered. "I hope I wouldn't panic in a situation like that. I hope I'd keep my wits about me and do what had to be done."

"Randi and Jon mentioned seeing an officer driving around their neighborhood shortly before their house was hit," Angie said.

"They said his name was Officer Pandy," Jenna said.

Chief Martin said, "Yes. He's one of the officers I'm working with from Silver Cove. They've beefed up patrolling the neighborhoods in the hope of deterring the arsonist. It obviously didn't work that night."

Angie told Chief Martin how she'd experienced an odd sensation when she saw a man walking away from the fire scene the other night. "We followed after him, but he was gone when we turned the corner."

"Angie thinks the guy might be the arsonist," Jenna said. She explained that it might be helpful to ask nearby businesses if they had security cameras trained on the sidewalks. "That way Angie could look through them to see if she spotted the man."

"Great idea," the chief said. "Was there anything about the guy that would stand out if he was in a crowd?"

"Really? Nothing." Angie frowned. "He looked like thousands of other guys around here. Average in height. Slim. Dark hair. Business casual clothes."

"But something about him gave you a bad feeling?" the chief asked.

"Yes," Angie said with a sinking feeling in her stomach. "It sure did."

10

Angie, Finch, and Courtney stepped onto the porch of Joan and Eugene Foster's home, the next door neighbors of Randi and Jon Willoughby, and were welcomed by a short, gray-haired woman with light blue eyes and a slightly taller man with white hair and sharp blue eyes. Both the man and woman were in their late-seventies.

"It's a pleasure to meet you," Joan said and shook hands with the three guests. "We saw you across the street on the night Randi and Jon's house burned."

"It was a very upsetting night," Eugene said with a shake of his head. "But thankfully, Randi and Jon got out safely. That's what matters."

Holding hands and slowly leading the way, the

couple invited the investigators into their neat, cozy living room where they all took comfortable seats around a fireplace. A pot of tea and a jug of ice water sat on a tray on the coffee table. Joan poured drinks while Eugene passed around a plate of cookies.

"Have you seen Randi and Jon since that night?" Angie asked.

"We have," Joan said. "They came by a few days after the fire to see if any of their belongings were salvageable. We invited them in for lunch."

"They told us they're going to have the house rebuilt and renovated so they can move back in," Eugene said. "I was thrilled to hear it."

"We love those two," Joan said. "They're wonderful neighbors. Always ready to lend a hand. We'll do whatever we can to help them."

Courtney asked, "Did you hear or see anything that night that might be considered suspicious?"

"We spoke with the police and with Randi and Jon," Joan said. "We told them there wasn't anything amiss that night. Not that we noticed anyway."

"No unusual odors?" Finch asked.

Joan and Eugene exchanged a quick glance. "No," they said in unison.

"What about sounds? Did you hear anything unexpected?" Courtney asked.

"We had our windows closed," Eugene explained. "We get chilled easily and it was a cold evening."

"Had you been outside earlier?" Finch asked.

"We had dinner in the kitchen, just hot dogs and baked beans," Joan told them. "Then we came in here to watch a movie. After that we went to bed. We were both reading when we saw the flashes of red outside the window. The fire had started next door." The woman poured more water into her husband's glass.

Eugene said, "At first, it simply didn't register what it was. We wondered if it was the lights on a police car parked in the street. I got up and looked outside. I saw the Willoughbys' house. Flames were shooting out of the windows, out of the roof. Joan called '911' and we hurried out to the porch to see where Randi and Jon were."

"My heart was pounding so hard I was sure it would burst through my chest." Joan put her hand over her heart and took in some deep breaths.

Eugene placed his arm protectively around his wife's shoulders and she seemed to calm. Joan went on. "We saw Randi rush out the side door of the house into the yard. We called to her, but she didn't hear us."

"Where did she go?" Angie asked.

"She ran into the backyard," Eugene said. "We didn't know it then, but Jon was stuck in the bedroom. The fire was just outside his bedroom door and the window was stuck. Randi smashed the window so Jon could escape."

"It was very lucky Randi was able to do that," Courtney said.

"Can you tell us a little about the neighborhood?" Angie asked hoping to get some information on the other people who lived nearby.

"We've lived here for about ten years," Joan said. "We had a huge house on the other side of Silver Cove. It was too much for us at that point in life. The kids were grown and out of the house. It was too much space for us. The yard was too big to care for anymore. We wanted something more manageable."

"So we looked for something smaller," Eugene sipped from his water glass. "And we found this house. It had just come on the market. We snatched it up. It was exactly what we were looking for."

Joan smiled. "One floor, a nice sized kitchen, and it has four bedrooms. We don't need all the bedrooms, but it's very nice to have the space when the kids come to visit."

"How many children do you have?" Finch asked.

"We have four kids," Joan said. "Two girls and two boys. We're very lucky. All smart kids."

Eugene said, "Lisa is a lawyer, Lorrie, our youngest, is an engineer, Miles is a professor, and Lincoln is a doctor. They're a great bunch. We're very fortunate."

Angie looked over to the table in front of a window that had framed photographs of the Foster family and smiled at the large family.

"The whole family is close," Joan told them. "Our kids all live outside of Boston, but they visit all the time or we go into the city for lunch or to see a show with them."

"Any grandkids?" Finch asked.

"We have eight," Joan beamed. "All the kids and grandkids are healthy and happy. Lorrie married young and got divorced after only a year, but she remarried a nice man and they've been together for five years."

"What happened between Lorrie and her first husband?" Angie asked.

Joan sighed. "I think it was a case of just getting married too soon. They started dating in middle school here in Silver Cove, and stayed together through high school. They got engaged as sopho- mores in college and married the following year. I don't think it was a good match. People change a good deal as they move through college and enter the work force. Lorrie and Dave grew apart. Thankfully, they didn't have any kids together."

"The divorce was amicable," Eugene said. "They both thought the divorce was for the best."

"What happened to Dave?" Angie asked.

"He became a salesman," Joan said with a smile. "He lives at the north end of Silver Cove. We see him occasionally, he always greets us warmly, as we do him."

"Did he remarry?"

"He did not. He works for his mother's company. The job keeps him busy," Eugene said. "He does live with a girlfriend, but I always hoped he would find someone he wanted to marry. It hasn't worked out that way yet."

"You grew up in Silver Cove?" Courtney asked.

"We did. I was three years ahead of Joan in school so we didn't really cross paths until college," Eugene said and his eyes brightened when he looked at his wife. "We ended up going to the same college and that's where we met. It was my lucky day." The man chuckled. "We met in Boston, not here in town which would seem the most likely place to run into each other."

"Did you both work?" Courtney questioned.

"Oh, yes. We both taught school for years and then we both moved up to principal positions," Joan said. "I worked at the high school here in town and Eugene worked at a middle school over in Princeton."

"We're fortunate," Eugene said. "Good pensions and great health insurance. At our ages, that's important."

Finch nodded in agreement. "And how is the neighborhood to live in?"

"There have been changes over the years," Eugene said. "Families and couples have come and gone, but it retains a feeling of community. You feel you can call on your neighbors, if you need to. People help out. We know most of the residents. We're close to a few couples, friendly with most, and some we know their names and wave to each other, but they're on the other side of the neighborhood and we don't run into them often."

"It sounds like a nice place to live," Angie said.

"Oh, it is." As soon as she said the words, Joan's expression changed to one of apprehension. "At least, it was."

Eugene took his wife's hand and patted it gently.

"It still *is* a nice place, and it will be even better once that arsonist is caught."

"The kids wanted us to come down to Boston until this mess has blown over," Joan said. "But, we like to sleep in our own beds, be around our own things. Eugene has a bad back and his balance isn't great. He has other health problems. Sometimes, I have insomnia. We don't move around like we once did. We're stiff, slow, sometimes unsteady. We have to be careful. We don't want to stay anyplace unfamiliar."

"We like it here," Eugene smiled. "It's home."

"Is there anyone in the neighborhood you might suspect could have set these fires?" Angie asked.

Joan's hand flew to her mouth and let out a little gasp.

"Someone *in* our neighborhood?" Eugene asked. "We ... we never...."

"We never considered such a thing," Joan finished her husband's sentence. "It can't be someone from here. It just can't. That would be too terrible."

Finch said gently, "Is there anyone in the neighborhood who behaves in a slightly odd manner? Maybe someone who doesn't act that friendly, maybe has a temper? Someone who seems unhappy or preoccupied or who doesn't quite fit in?"

"I can't think of anyone," Joan said softly.

"Have your kids or grandkids had any issues or trouble with anyone?" Angie asked.

Eugene shook his head and then looked at his wife. "I don't think so."

Joan said, "There hasn't been any trouble with anyone."

"Do you know Officer Pandy?" Courtney asked.

Joan nodded. "Yes, we do. He works for the Silver Cove Police Department. He and some other officers take turns driving through the neighborhood checking to make sure everything is okay."

"Officer Pandy lives at the edge of this neighborhood, down near the state park. He swings through here whenever he can. We hoped the police presence would deter the arsonist, but he must have learned the police officers' routines. Maybe he watched for a while and figured out when the officers wouldn't be around. Maybe he knew when it would be safe to set Randi's and Jon's house on fire."

Angie felt like her blood had just froze in her veins. *If the arsonist was able to learn the routines and schedules of the police and their drive-thrus, wouldn't that mean the person was around the neighborhood a lot? Did the arsonist live in this neighborhood?*

Panic raced over Angie's skin. "Do you keep your outside lights on all night?"

Eugene took his wife's hand in his and held it tightly. "Yes. Yes, we do."

"Good. Make sure they're on when you turn in for the night."

11

—————

Late in the afternoon, Jenna and Angie met Chief Martin at the Silver Cove Police Department to view some security tapes taken from several businesses located near the building that went up in flames.

The three sat hunched over a laptop screen watching two hours of various videos. Most showed scenes of people walking past the stores and of customers entering and leaving shops. The night footage was more difficult to make out and some of the film was grainy or foggy looking. Angie was looking for the man at the fire who had given her a bad feeling.

When the last of the tapes ran on the screen,

Angie pushed back and sighed. "I didn't notice the man I saw that night. Maybe he's on the tape, but I just can't make him out. I'm sorry. I was hopeful I'd spot him."

"It's okay," the chief said. "It was worth a shot. Most of the time, video footage doesn't pan out. One of the detectives who is also working on the case told us that a fingerprint was discovered on a back window of the business building. A lot of the windows had blown out from the fire, but this one was at ground level and an officer noticed a smudge. It turned out to be a viable fingerprint. Of course, it could have been from someone other than the arsonist, but they ran it through the databases looking for a match."

"Did they get one?" Jenna asked.

The chief said, "They did not. However, if a suspect does turn up, the police will check to see if his prints match the ones on this window. That would put the suspect at the building. It's not definitive, of course, but it's something."

"That's very good," Angie said. "Maybe finger-prints will be found at the other fire scenes and they'll match this one."

"We'll keep our fingers crossed," the chief said.

UNDER A BRIGHT BLUE SKY, Jenna and Angie walked along the busy sidewalk in the center of Silver Cove. The town was well-known as a place for artists to thrive and there were plenty of shops along the main street selling paintings, fabrics, sculpture, yarn, handcrafted jewelry, and other fine crafts. Unlike Sweet Cove which drew the tourist crowd, Silver Cove was more of a residential town. Tourists found their way there, but the town lacked inns and hotels and the coast was rocky without any wide sandy beaches so fewer out-of-towners visited the pretty place.

The sisters arrived at a restaurant that stood next to the business building that had been set on fire several nights ago and they entered into the modern space where the owner was waiting for them. Mickey Smith greeted the young women and led them to the far corner of the dining room that was still being set up for lunch.

After preliminary conversation, Angie asked, "Can you tell us about the night?"

"Sure," Mickey said. "I'll tell you, I never want to relive a night like that one. I was certain the restaurant would catch fire. I bought the place three months ago. My heart was in my throat watching that darned fire. I hoped and prayed my building would be saved. By some miracle, we're still standing and are fully operational."

"We're so glad for you," Jenna said. "It must have been a nightmare."

"A nightmare times a thousand," Mickey said. "I still feel panicky whenever I think about it."

"You were open for business that night?" Angie asked.

"We were, but we got closed down by the fire department and the police. They didn't think it was safe for us to be doing business as usual so we boxed up people's dinners and sent them on their way. I stepped outside and nearly fainted dead away when I saw the blaze. No wonder the authorities told us to close the store for the night." Mickey shook his head in amazement.

"Did you notice anything that seemed off that night?" Jenna asked.

"We were super busy. I didn't notice anything except for what was under my nose right in here."

"What about a funny odor? Did anyone complain of a strange odor?"

"Not to my knowledge. What would an odor indicate?"

"Perhaps the use of an accelerant," Angie told the man.

Mickey's face almost paled. "Has accelerant been used in the other fires?"

"Not that we know of," Angie said. "But that doesn't mean the arsonist's mode of operation will remain the same."

"I see," Mickey said with worry in his tone.

"Can you tell us if anyone was around who was sort of troubled?" Jenna asked. "Did anyone behave strangely or aggressively? Did you see anyone upset or agitated or angry?"

"Well, when you run a restaurant, especially one with a bar, then you do see stuff like that, people who are not always at their best." Mickey looked off across the room. "That night, though? I don't recall any issues that night."

"How about the night before? Or maybe within the past week?"

"Nothing that stands out. The usual drunks. A few arguments. A few breakups. Nothing violent. Nothing out of the ordinary."

"You don't have a regular customer who comes in and might be a little difficult?" Angie asked.

"Not really," Mickey said. "The bartenders and waitstaff have a meeting with me once or twice a week. They tell me if things are weird or if something happens that bothers them. I ask them to be upfront with me. To let me know when things aren't right. I want good working conditions here for my employees."

"Do you know the accountant who owned the business on the first floor of the building?" Jenna questioned.

"I do, sure. Morris Humphrey. A nice guy. He comes in here for lunch or dinner quite often."

"Did he seem worried or nervous about anything? Did he tell you about anyone who might be angry with him?" Angie asked.

"Nothing like that. Morris seemed normal. I haven't seen him since the fire." Mickey gave a shake of his head. "That thing sure went up fast, didn't it? Scared the heck out of me, I'll tell you that. You never know, do you? One day, business is booming, the next day the place is leveled by fire. One day, you're riding high, the next you're flat on the ground. It kind of takes some of your confidence away."

Jenna and Angie went from business to business asking questions about the night of the fire. No one saw anything. Nobody heard anything. It was like the arsonist had been invisible, moving through town like a ghost.

As they were leaving the last place, a high-end clothing shop, a salesclerk came up to them.

"Excuse me." The young woman looked to be in her late teens. She had long brown hair and brown eyes, high cheekbones, and a athlete's slender body. "I heard you talking to the owner."

A strange sensation fluttered over Angie's skin. "Yes?"

"You're asking about the fire?" the teen asked.

"Were you working that night?" Jenna asked.

"Yeah, I was. We closed at ten and I stayed a little longer to help straighten up and make some notes for the day staff about low inventory. I couldn't believe what was going on outside."

"Did you stick around to watch?" Angie asked.

"For about thirty minutes. I was across from the fire on the other side of the street. The heat was pretty intense. The police started to move us further away from the activity ... in case the fire spread."

"Did you notice anything before the fire started?" Jenna asked.

"What do you mean?" the young woman asked.

"Were you out back? Did you happen to see

anyone suspicious lurking around before the fire started?"

"No, I didn't."

Jenna decided the conversation wasn't going to lead to anything and was about to finish up with the discussion when she noticed the look on Angie's face.

"Did you notice anything or see anything odd while the fire was blazing?" Angie asked with a hoarse voice.

"I ... well, I don't know." The teenager pushed her hair behind her ear.

"What did you notice?" Angie asked.

"I was walking up the sidewalk. A guy bumped into me. He was walking the other way."

Angie's heart pounded. "What about him?"

"He bumped into me with his shoulder. He mustn't have been watching where he was going. He smelled like alcohol. A lot of alcohol."

"What did he look like?"

"Pretty average. Dark hair, a beard. An average-looking face. He wasn't wearing a suit and tie, but he sort of looked like a businessman. He had on a collared shirt and well-pressed, nicer slacks."

"Heavy? Slim?" Angie asked.

"More on the slim side."

"What about him?" Jenna asked. "Why do you bring him up?"

"He smelled of a lot of booze. He said some things to me about the fire. He was smiling. It seemed odd, like he was enjoying it. He made me uncomfortable." The young woman raised a shoulder. "I don't know why I'm telling you this."

"Did you see where the man went?" Angie asked.

"I started away from him. I got the impression he was going to keep talking about the fire. He was all excited. I wanted to go home so I said something like *have a good night*. I wanted to get away from him. I headed off and he kept walking in the opposite direction than I was going."

Angie introduced herself and Jenna to the teenager.

"I'm Anna Billings. I work here a few times a week after school."

"Would you be willing to speak with a police officer about your experience?" Angie asked. "Would you tell him about this man who bumped into you?"

"Really?" Anna's eyes went wide and her facial muscles tensed. "I don't think it's anything important."

"The officer is our friend." Angie told the girl Chief Martin's name. "I think he'd be very interested to hear what you have to say about this man. It might prove to be very helpful to the case."

Anna moved nervously from foot to foot. "I guess so. I guess I could talk to him. If you think it would help."

I do, Angie thought. *I think it could be a big help.*

12

A ngie and her sisters looked through the clothing racks of gowns for bridesmaids' dresses for the wedding. "I think a dusty rose color or maybe, lavender, would be pretty," she said.

"What about this one?" Courtney held up a long strapless dress that would hug the chest and then flow softly to the floor.

"I don't like it," Jenna said. "I think I'd be tugging at the top of the dress all the time to make sure it wasn't about to fall off. I'd rather have something with straps or a halter top."

"I agree," Ellie said. "Even if there are only spaghetti straps, it would make me feel more secure."

Angie held up two more dresses. "What do you think of these?"

"Ooh." Courtney lifted one of the hangers from her sister's hand and held the dress up to herself. "I like this one. It seems sophisticated, but it isn't tight over the hips. I think it would be really comfortable. And it isn't strapless."

"The color is pretty." Jenna touched the skirt of the dress and brought it to the side to see how it would move."

"The fabric is great," Ellie told them. "It will move softly when we walk. It's very feminine."

"Want to try it on?" Angie asked her sisters.

Jenna, Courtney, and Ellie searched the rack for their sizes and took the dresses to the fitting room where they put them on. Angie sat in a white cushioned chair waiting for her sisters' fashion show and when the three came out, her breath caught in her throat and she put her hand to the side of her face.

"Oh." Angie's throat was tight, but she managed to say, "You all look so beautiful. The dress looks great on all three of you."

"I think we look terrific," Jenna admired herself and her two sisters in the full-length mirror. "It suits all of us."

"What do you think, sis? Do we have a winner?" Courtney asked.

"Definitely. I can't believe we found the dresses so fast."

"We're very efficient," Ellie smiled. "And we all agree, too."

"Do you want to keep looking just to be sure?" Jenna asked.

Angie shook her head. "No. This is the one. You'll just have to choose shoes and then come back to have the dresses shortened."

They paid for the gowns and decided to have the store hold them so they could return with shoes for the alterations.

Stepping out onto Main Street, Courtney suggested, "Want to go look at shoes? We found the dresses so quickly, we have plenty of time to go shoe shopping."

As they were heading up the brick sidewalk towards the shoe store, Angie's phone buzzed.

Courtney sighed and said to her sisters, "Why do I think our shopping trip has come to an abrupt end?"

"It's a text from Chief Martin," Angie said. "He's going to the Willoughbys' house in Silver Cove to meet an investigator to go over the windows looking for fingerprints. They're hoping to find some to match to the prints found on the window at the business that burned. He wants to know if any of us can go along."

"I'll go," Courtney said. "Even though I would rather look at shoes."

"Me, too," Jenna agreed.

"I don't think I should join you," Ellie said. "Who knows how long you'll be? I'm meeting with a couple of B and B guests in a couple of hours."

"It's okay," Angie told Ellie. "The three of us will go. You go and meet with your guests."

Chief Martin swung by the shops and picked up the three Roselands, and then he drove the short distance to Silver Cove.

Standing on the sidewalk in front of the fire-ravaged home of Randi and Jon Willoughby, Jenna, Courtney, and Angie stared in silence at the ruined building. The wood was black on the front of the house especially near the windows where the fire had burst through the glass.

"It still stinks of burning," Courtney noted, her nostrils flaring.

"It sure is a mess." Jenna looked from side to side at the charred ruins, the shattered glass, the part of the roof that had collapsed. "Is it worth trying to fix it? Maybe it would be better to knock it down and build a new house."

"It sure is a sad sight." A pang squeezed at Angie's heart. "Poor Randi and Jon. Everything they owned must be lost. Photographs, mementos, things that can't ever be replaced."

"The couple is remarkably resilient," Chief Martin said. "They're bound and determined to rebuild and reclaim their home."

Courtney's face hardened. "We need to catch this arsonist, and we need to catch him soon ... before he can hurt anyone else."

"Then let's go talk to the investigator," the chief gestured to the backyard. "Simmons is an expert in gathering and analyzing fingerprints."

When they made their way around to the back of the house, they spotted a small, older man with gray hair and dark-rimmed glasses kneeling on the ground leaning over half of a window.

Chief Martin called to the man and Simmons's head snapped up to see who had arrived. Simmons pointed to the glass in the broken window. "I'm sorry to say I'm not having any luck here. I hoped for a partial print, but I haven't found one yet."

Simmons stood and shook hands with the sisters. "I hoped for more, but when a fire is involved, it is very difficult to recover any viable prints. The water, the soot, the collapsed parts of a building, it all combines to make discovery and recovery near impossible. I'll head to the front and sides now, if you'd like to tag along."

Chief Martin quietly suggested that the sisters wander around the grounds and circle the house. "You can try and pick up on something. Maybe you'll sense something?"

"We'll try," Angie said. "When a violent act is committed, things can remain and float on the air."

"Okay. Good." The chief really had no idea what Angie meant, but he hoped it would lead to a clue so he left the Roselands alone to do what they did and he went to catch up with Mr. Simmons.

"Shall we split up?" Jenna asked.

"Sure," Angie said. "I'll take the side that faces the neighbors, Eugene and Joan Foster."

"I'll stay back here," Courtney said as she began to walk slowly around the rear yard.

"I'll do the other side." Jenna headed away. "We can meet at the front and look around the lawn and the front periphery of the home."

Angie stepped to the side adjacent to the Fosters' place and began to move slowly over the grass looking for any tiny thing that might become a clue.

Some glass from the second floor crunched under Angie's feet as she attempted to clear her head in order to focus on the task of trying to sense something that went on here the other night.

Why would someone do this? What was the goal? Revenge? Attention? Power and control? Thumbing a nose at law enforcement?

There was a trace of humidity in the air that made Angie feel hot and sweaty and out-of-sorts.

I bet he came from behind. I bet the arsonist hid in the woods until he was ready to start the fire. He didn't use an accelerant. How did he set the fire? Matches?

A woman's voice called her name and Angie looked up to see Joan Foster on her front porch waving at her. Angie walked over to the Fosters' yard.

"I thought it was you," Joan said. She was wearing tan capri pants and a white short-sleeve shirt. "Is there any news?"

"None, I'm afraid," Angie told her. "We're just having another look around the property. It's easy to miss things the first time."

"I understand. It must be painstaking work," Joan said. "Eugene is inside napping. I decided to come out on the porch for a while. The smell from the fire is still pretty bad though."

Angie agreed. "It will help to get rid of the odor

when the construction crew comes to remove the burned sections of the house. Is Eugene okay?"

"Oh, sure. He just gets tired, that's all. He's been using his wheelchair more the past few days. His health isn't the greatest, heart problems, diabetes, high blood pressure. The man is a wreck." Joan moved her hand in the air. "Getting old is for the birds. I don't know what I'd do without that old bugger. He's the only man I've ever loved. He better stick around for a while longer."

Angie's heart squeezed. "How long have you been married?"

"Fifty-five years next month." Joan smiled. "I'd like fifty-five more years with that husband of mine. But don't tell him I said that. He'll get a big head."

"I'm getting married next month," Angie said.

"What date?" Joan asked.

The woman's eyebrows raised when Angie told her. "That's our wedding date, too."

"Is it? What a coincidence."

"I wish you a long and happy marriage, my dear. I hope your husband is as wonderful as my Eugene."

"I think he's pretty special." Angie's eyes were bright.

Joan's face clouded. "We ran into our ex-son-in-law yesterday."

Angie saw the woman's changed expression. "Was something wrong?"

With a sigh, Joan pushed a strand of gray-white hair out of her eyes. "I feel badly for Dave. Things just don't seem to go his way. He had a live-in girlfriend for about half a year. She moved out a couple of weeks ago. Dave was upset, of course. He tried to downplay the breakup, but Eugene and I could see the hurt in his eyes. Even though he and our daughter divorced, I still can feel sorry for Dave. I don't think it's healthy for people to be alone."

A wave of unease washed over Angie. "What did you say Dave did for work?"

"He's a salesman. He works for his mother's company here in Silver Cove."

"What company does she own?"

"Belting Auto Supply. They sell automotive supplies to dealerships and garages. They do very well." Joan looked over to the Willoughbys' front lawn. "There's your sister."

Angie glanced over her shoulder, nodded to Jenna, and turned to the older woman. "I need to get back. Nice talking to you, Mrs. Foster. Give my best to your husband." Before she took two steps towards the burned out house, Angie turned back. "Are you still keeping the porch lights on every night?"

"Yes, we are. We both make sure they're on before we go to bed. We keep the front and the back porch lights on all night long."

A sudden flash of red flared in Angie's vision for a second. She rubbed at her temple with shaky fingers and took in a long breath. "Okay. Good. Stay safe."

13

_____

Wearing an apron and with her hair up in a loose bun, Angie stood at the kitchen island adding ingredients into a mixing bowl for a cocoa cream pie. "And then I saw a flash of red, but the flash was only in my head. It worries me. Do you think Eugene and Joan are in danger?"

Jenna, Tom, and Josh sat at the island across from Angie.

"I don't like the sound of it." Josh handed the whisk to his fiancée. "Your intuition is trying to tell you something."

"I'll tell Chief Martin." Angie whisked the batter a little too vigorously.

"Maybe ease up on the pie filling," Jenna kidded

her sister. "It doesn't deserve to be handled so fiercely."

"Oh." Angie set down the whisk. "Right."

Tom took a swallow from his beer glass and warned his sister-in-law, "You might also want to watch what you're thinking while you bake, Angie. You know what can happen."

Whenever Angie baked something she had to be very careful what she was thinking because her thoughts and intentions could be transferred to the sweets she was preparing. Usually, she kept a positive and cheerful frame of mind when she worked so that only good thoughts would be transferred into the bakery items and passed on to her customers.

"You're right. I can't think about arson while I'm baking." She took a deep breath before continuing.

Jenna's eyes went wide. "Wow, the results of that could be very dangerous. Clear your thoughts before you pick up that whisk."

Angie stepped back from the counter and wiped her hands on her apron. "Joan told me about her ex-son-in-law, Dave. His live-in girlfriend recently left him. Joan and Eugene ran into Dave at a store. She said he was visibly upset. I got a weird feeling when she was talking about Dave."

"What's Dave's profile?" Josh asked. "Do you

know anything about him? Does his background and experience match up with the profile of an arsonist?"

Angie swallowed hard. "I don't know much. Dave is a salesman for his mother's auto supply company. He is divorced from Eugene's and Joan's daughter. He never remarried. His recent girlfriend just moved out."

Tom rested his arms on the counter top. "You might learn some things about Dave if you interview his former girlfriend."

"That's a good point," Jenna said. "Would Chief Martin let us talk to her, do you think? Dave isn't a suspect. Angie just had a strange feeling when she and Joan talked about him."

"Well," Tom said with a devious smile, "you could always sort of run into her."

"I wonder where Dave was on the night of the fires," Josh said with a serious expression.

"Probably home alone in his apartment," Jenna said. "The girlfriend hadn't moved out before the first few fires, but it doesn't mean she was at home on those evenings. I bet it's likely there isn't anyone who could vouch for Dave being at home ... if that's where he tells us he was."

"Chief Martin might want to look into Dave's

whereabouts," Angie suggested. "I'll talk to him."

Angie's phone buzzed on the kitchen table and Jenna got up to get it for her sister.

"My hands are covered in flour. Could you see who it's from?" Angie asked.

Jenna checked and then lifted her eyes to the others. "It's Chief Martin. He says there's a *situation*. He asks if some of us can come. He gives an address. It's in Silver Cove."

"Oh, no." Angie's face paled.

"Shall the four of us go?" Tom asked. "I can drive."

"I'd like it if you all came." Angie hurried to the sink to wash her hands while Jenna put the pie ingredients into the refrigerator, and then they all piled into Tom's car.

THE ADDRESS the chief gave Angie in the text was a small assisted living facility on the outskirts of Silver Cove. Police cars, fire trucks, and two ambulances were parked askew in front of the place. A crowd had gathered to watch and several members of the media stood on the periphery of the action interviewing people.

Chief Martin stood in the circular driveway of the building speaking with two officers and a firefighter.

The right side of the facility was a charred ruin.

When the chief spotted Angie, Jenna, and the men, he strode towards them, his face drawn and sad.

"Two elderly residents are dead," he told them with a hoarse voice. "Smoke inhalation seems to be the cause. Three other elderly, two men and a woman, have been injured and transported to the hospital."

"It was set?" Jenna asked to clarify.

"It was." The chief's jaw twitched slightly as he clenched his teeth, his eyes wandering over the damage. "The fire moved fast. The staff had trouble moving the people out of the facility quickly enough. Now the arsonist can add *murderer* to his resume."

"He's escalated," Angie said softly, thinking to herself. "What will he do next?"

"Why don't you look around at the crowd," Josh suggested as he put his arm around Angie. "See if you notice the man from the other night who made you feel uneasy."

"Good idea." Angie reached up and squeezed

Josh's hand. As she scanned the people in the crowd, she told the chief about the strange flash of red she saw when at Eugene and Joan Foster's house, and then she reported what Joan said about her ex-son-in-law."

"Interesting stuff." The chief stroked his chin. "I'll tell Officer Pandy it might be a good idea to up the police presence in the Foster's neighborhood. Can you ask Mrs. Foster what Dave's most recent girlfriend's name is?"

"Sure. What should I tell her when Mrs. Foster asks me why I want to know?" Angie asked.

"Say something like it might be possible the woman saw a person of interest near the office building that burned. If you get the name, it might be a good idea to have a talk with the woman. Ask some questions about Dave without being accusatory. See what she's got to say. Depending on what you learn, it might be prudent for me or Officer Pandy to talk with her."

"Phillip!" An officer yelled to Chief Martin and as he hurried over to see what was wrong, a pulse of adrenaline rushed through Angie's veins.

"Something's up." Jenna watched the officer speak animatedly to the chief.

A police car left the scene with squealing tires

and raced off down the street.

"Uh, oh," Angie muttered.

The chief ran past them to his car. "Another fire. Belmont Street. Meet me there."

The foursome moved quickly down the sidewalk to Tom's truck.

"Two fires in one night?" Jenna asked, bewildered by it all. "He's really ramping up."

"Two people are dead because of this guy," Angie said with anger in her voice. "Why aren't there any clues? Why can't anyone do something to stop him?"

"You're all working hard on this," Josh said. "You or the police will catch a break soon. One little thing will be all it takes."

Tom moved the steering wheel and the truck careened around a corner sending his passengers tilting in their seats. "Sorry."

When he pulled the truck to halt at the end of Belmont Street, they all stared at the small Cape, fully engulfed by flames.

"Look at that," Jenna whispered.

"I've never seen anything like it." Tom gazed in amazement at the flames shooting high into the sky.

They climbed out and started down the dark sidewalk of the usually quiet neighborhood and stood about three houses away from the scene.

"Look around," Jenna quietly told her twin. "Look at the people gathered to watch. The arsonist might be here."

Scanning the crowd, Angie noticed a wide-eyed look on three of the young men whose faces were locked onto the goings-on. Pointing them out to her sister, she said, "The one in the red sweatshirt looks especially eager about the fire."

Jenna spotted the young man Angie had pointed at and narrowed her eyes. "He sure does. Is he eager because of the commotion in the usually sleepy neighborhood? Or is there another reason?"

"Let's go find out," Tom led the way to stand next to the guy and struck up a conversation. "You live around here? Whose house is on fire?"

The tall brown-haired man was around twenty-five-years old. "Yeah, I live over there." He gestured to a blue house on the corner and then pointed to the burning house. "That house belongs to the Madisons."

"How many people live there?" Tom asked.

"Three. A couple and a little kid."

"Did they get out safely?" Josh asked.

"Somebody told me they're with the EMTs."

"Are they okay?" Josh pushed for more information.

"Not sure." The young guy ran his hand over his short hair.

"I smell booze on that guy's breath," Angie whispered to Jenna.

"At least, we know where he lives if we need to take a look at him," Jenna answered. "Are you *sensing* anything?"

"I'm a bundle of nerves. I feel like I can't concentrate."

"I feel the same way," Jenna sighed. "Is the actual fire blocking us somehow?"

"What do you mean?" Angie asked.

"Is the power of the fire so strong that it interferes with our ability to feel something?"

Angie stood with her mouth slightly open, thinking about what Jenna had said. "Chief Martin told us it's difficult to solve cases of arson because any clues are burned up. Does the fire also burn away anything that we might sense lingering on the air?"

"Is that why we can't figure anything out?" Jenna asked. "How can we figure out how to keep the fire from blocking us?"

Angie gave a shrug and turned her palms face up. "I have no idea."

14

After leaving Belmont Street around 9pm to head home, Angie and Jenna were feeling low and useless and were racking their brains for ways to discover some clues.

"Doesn't the older couple, Eugene and Joan, live nearby here," Tom asked.

"Three streets over," Angie said.

"Why don't we take a ride by their house," Josh suggested. "Check that everything's okay."

Tom turned the truck to the right instead of going left on the road back to Sweet Cove and drove slowly past the Willoughbys' blackened home.

"What a mess." Tom couldn't believe his eyes.

"How can a person do this?" Josh asked. "What's missing inside someone that allows him to cause such destruction? To ruin other's people's lives. Is it rage at the world? Is that what does this?"

No one could answer the question.

Angie spotted Eugene standing at his front door staring with a scowl at the unknown truck moving towards his house.

"Can you stop for a second?" Angie got out of the car when Tom pulled to the curb. "It's me, Mr. Foster. Are you okay?"

"Oh, it's you, Angie." Eugene breathed a sigh of relief. "I didn't recognize the truck. I wondered who was driving around the neighborhood. We're okay."

Jenna, Tom, and Josh emerged and headed over to talk to the older man just as Joan opened the door to the porch. Her face lit up when she saw who was there.

"We didn't go over to Belmont Street," Joan told them. "We didn't want to see it. It's all too much."

Eugene said, "The neighbors told us that the Madisons are shaken and upset, but are unhurt. We're very thankful for that."

"The house on the other hand is a total loss," Joan said. "Were you there? Did you see it? Do you agree?"

"We don't have the experience to know for sure," Angie said. Wanting to turn the conversation to something more uplifting, she introduced Tom and Josh to the couple.

"You're Angie's fiancé," Joan said to Josh as she stepped forward to shake his hand. "And you're Jenna's husband. Two fine men. You're lucky to have these women in your lives." Joan looked to Angie and Jenna. "And you two young women have found wonderful men." Moving to Eugene, the older woman clutched his arm and rested her head on her husband's shoulder. "Just like my wonderful Eugene."

BEFORE LEAVING the Victorian for a meeting at the police station, Angie and Josh met the delivery truck and instructed the men which rooms to place the new furniture in.

"The third floor? No elevator?" One of the men asked with downturned lips.

"Sorry," Angie told him.

Euclid and Circe followed the delivery men up and down the staircase watching them closely to be sure they didn't damage any of the things.

"These cats don't miss a trick, do they?" The

second man asked. "I wouldn't want them watching me all day long."

"You get used to it," Mr. Finch told them.

When everything was in place in Angie's and Josh's new apartment, they headed up to check it out.

Euclid sat on the new sofa and Circe was in the bedroom gently padding over the new mattress.

Josh let out a hearty laugh and asked the cats, "Does everything check out?"

Euclid turned his nose to the ceiling and let out a loud meow. Circe curled up on the bed and purred.

"I'll take that as a *yes*," Josh said as he put his arm around Angie's shoulders. "I'm going to love living here."

Angie eyed her fiancé. "Because of the cats ... or because of me?"

With a wide grin, Josh said, "Well, both."

Circe trilled at Josh's remark.

ANGIE WALKED into the Sweet Cove Police Department and headed for the conference room where Chief Martin met her and introduced her to Silver Cove Officer Lou Pandy. Pandy was unable to attend his own department's briefing so he came down to Sweet Cove.

"I feel like I know you already." In his early forties, Pandy was six feet tall, slim, with brown hair and dark eyes. "Phillip speaks highly of you and your family. You all seem to have the natural abilities needed to work a crime. I understand you've been invaluable in the solving of several mysteries."

Angie flashed a look at Chief Martin and he shook his head quickly from side to side assuring the young woman that he had not breathed a word to Pandy about anyone's paranormal skills.

Taking seats around the conference table, the chief opened a folder and reviewed what was known about the fires. "The last two fires, set on the same night, were the worst in their ferocity. Two people at the assisted living place lost their lives and the house on Belmont Street is a complete loss. It will be bull-dozed once the investigators have finished with it."

"The arsonist has stepped up his game," Pandy said with a serious expression. "We need to step up to beat this guy."

"What does research into arson tell us will happen next?" Angie asked.

"The events will continue to heighten," the chief said, "but not to the degree of his recent escalation.

J. A. WHITING

He may continue to set two fires in one evening, but it is unlikely he will jump to setting more than two at one time. That might take a few weeks."

"I suppose we have to be thankful for that," Angie said.

"His targets might become more visible, however," the chief said. "He won't be satisfied with setting only a single family house on fire. The targets will become more visible, more public, like the assisted living facility. A bigger audience will be wanted. A more impressive fire will be needed to provide the arsonist with some satisfaction."

"Like what?" Angie asked. "A hospital? A big building?"

"Possibly," Pandy said. "City Hall, a school, the police department. He'd love to hit a fire station or a police headquarters to thumb his nose at us."

"The arsonist is becoming bolder," the chief said. "He might set fires during the day, he might set fires in public spaces where a lot of people are around. He might start to feel invincible ... which will make him more dangerous."

"And then, he'll slip up," Angie said. "He'll make a mistake. A mistake that will lead us right to him."

"We can hope," the chief said. "The investigators found something at the fire on Belmont Street. The

140

arsonist used an accelerant this time. He must have wanted to inflict more damage than usual."

Angie's face tightened and her heart pounded.

"The accelerant was put inside of a beer bottle."

"A beer bottle?" Pandy asked.

Angie leaned forward.

"It was a craft beer. An expensive one. A lot of people drink it, but a lot of people don't."

"That's good then," Angie said. "It narrows the field."

"Not quite enough," the chief said. "But, we'll take what we can get."

"What brand of beer was it?" Pandy asked.

"High Stars."

Pandy's eyes widened. "I drink that from time to time. It's one of my favorites. Too expensive though. This is the first time a bottle with accelerant was used," the officer noted.

The chief nodded. "That's right. It might be interesting if it's used again, especially if it's in the same kind of beer bottle. As far as fingerprints, there haven't been any prints left at any of the other scenes. There could have been some left behind, but that evidence has been destroyed by the fire or by the fighting of the fire. So no luck there."

Angie and Pandy both nodded.

"There have also been no witnesses. No one has seen a fire being set. No one has seen anyone running from a fire. We do have a young woman who works part time in a clothing store on Main Street in Silver Cove who ran into a man on the evening the business building was set ablaze. She reports the man smelled like alcohol, that he seemed overly excited by the fire. He made her uncomfortable."

"It doesn't mean he's the arsonist," Pandy said with a shrug.

"The chances are low that this particular guy is our man," the chief said. "But he could be."

"When I met the salesclerk, I didn't ask her how old she thought the man was," Angie said.

"She said it was hard to judge his age," Chief Martin answered. "She estimated him to be anywhere from his early twenties into his thirties."

"That's a wide range," Pandy said just as his phone buzzed with a text. The man sighed when he read it. "It's my wife. I need to call her. It's about our son. Again." Pandy got up and left the room.

"Family trouble?" Angie asked the chief when Pandy had closed the conference room door.

"Pandy's son is giving them a run for their money. He was in college, but he dropped out. That's not exactly accurate. The kid had all Ds and Fs in his courses. The college suggested he take a semester or two off."

"Does the son have trouble with academics or is he not applying himself?"

"I get the impression the kid is smart, but doesn't want to work too hard. Pandy's son has had two jobs in two months. He got fired from both of them."

"Why?" Angie asked.

"He gets to work late, leaves early, goofs off on the job," the chief said. "It's a mess. The kid drinks too much. Pandy suspects some drugs."

"It sounds like the kid is sabotaging himself."

Chief Martin said, "Pandy says he and his son don't get along. The kid has no respect for him."

"It seems the young man doesn't have any respect for himself," Angie said.

"Pandy told me the tension in the household is putting a strain on the marriage. I feel for the guy. He's having a rough time."

The beer bottle used at the fire scene popped into Angie's mind. *High Stars.* One of Pandy's favorites. Hmm.

15

A ngie and Jenna walked into Francine's stained glass shop in the center of Sweet Cove. Francine greeted her friends with a beaming smile and hugs. The woman, in her fifties, was slim with blond shoulder-length hair and emerald green eyes.

"What about some tea or a latte?" Francine had a tea kettle and a coffee machine in her backroom.

The sisters requested lattes and Francine was back in a jiffy, carrying a small tray with three hot drinks. "How are the wedding plans coming along?"

"Surprisingly well for someone who waited until the last minute to do everything." Jenna winked.

"It's not the last minute," Angie protested. "There are still a few weeks to go."

Francine and Jenna exchanged a look.

"It *is* the last minute," Francine agreed with Jenna with a chuckle.

"Angie's wearing our mother's bridal gown," Jenna said. "Ellie is making a few minor tweaks to it."

"You're lucky to have a sister who has seamstress skills."

The women talked about what was new and then Francine asked, "What about those fires?" Francine lived in a lovely home in Silver Cove where she had a stained glass workshop and showroom. "Sometimes, I can't sleep at night I'm so worried someone will set my place on fire."

"Keep all the outside lights on," Angie told her. "It makes it harder for an arsonist to set a fire."

"Okay, thanks for the tip." Worry still showed on the woman's face. "Maybe I should get a dog, or two."

The sisters knew Francine was kidding, but who could blame her for considering the idea.

Francine took a sip of her drink. "How I wish the police would catch this guy. What kind of a mind must someone have who does such things? Two people died the other night because of this nut. It's not just damage to homes and businesses. Now it's murder."

The women discussed the reasons why it was so difficult to catch an arsonist.

"I'm glad I'm not a police officer," Francine said. "The pressure must be terrible."

"I met Officer Pandy from Silver Cove the other day," Angie said. "Chief Martin introduced us."

"Pandy seems like a good guy," Francine said with a nod. "He seems to take his job seriously, but the man appears to have a kind side to him. I've seen him interact with shady characters. He's always calm and reasonable."

"He's been working very long hours on the case," Angie reported. "It has him quite upset."

"I hate to hear that. Things aren't easy at home. Pandy has some issues with his son," Francine said.

"How do you know this?" Jenna asked.

"I know his wife, Marine. She's a nice woman, friendly, personable. She works at the Rusty Anchor. Marine sometimes confides in me about the family troubles."

"I heard the son is a handful," Angie said.

"More than a handful," Francine told them. "Noah is extremely difficult. I guess he's been a little odd since he was a toddler. Tantrums, fits, he can't control his anger. He blames his parents for everything that goes wrong. Did you hear Noah got kicked out of college?"

"I heard he was asked to take a couple of semesters off," Angie said.

"Yeah, and the parents did not get a refund for the half of the semester Noah missed." Francine shook her head. "Marine told me how much tension and stress their son causes them. It's sad. They've done counseling, worked with a psychiatrist. Nothing seems to stem Noah's issues."

"Have you met Noah?" Jenna questioned.

"A few times. He always comes across as polite and pleasant. He isn't like that with his parents or brother. Noah does not get along with his parents, especially his dad."

"I heard he's been fired from a couple of jobs?" Angie asked.

"More than a couple." Francine rolled her eyes. "Noah can't get up early so he gets to work late. He can be sullen on the job. He doesn't take the work seriously. He's been fired twice in only a couple of months' time. Marine is beside herself. Noah won't take her suggestions, he's rude to his father. They don't know what to do."

"How does Noah do in school?" Jenna asked. "Does he work to his ability?"

"Gosh, no. The young man is smart, really smart. Noah doesn't take schoolwork seriously either. He gets poor grades despite being so smart."

"Does Noah have something he'd like to do for work?" Jenna asked.

"He'd like to be a firefighter, but that's out of the question," Francine said.

Hearing that Noah wanted to be a firefighter sent a feeling of anxiety rushing through Angie's body.

Francine said, "Noah would never be accepted for firefighting with his poor academic and work history, and he's too unreliable. Marine said she wondered if anyone would even write a recommendation for him."

"What about going to school to learn a trade?" Jenna asked. "Tom runs his own renovation and construction business. He likes to work with hands. He could never be stuck behind a desk all day. Maybe something like that would appeal to Noah?"

"Or maybe being a plumber or electrician?" Angie asked. "Maybe the young man hasn't found himself yet. Maybe he doesn't really know himself yet."

Francine sighed. "I hope one of these days he can

pull it together and make a turnaround … for both his *and* his parents' sakes."

Angie brought up Joan and Eugene Foster and explained how she'd met them.

Francine's eyes sparkled. "I know the Fosters. Such good people. They're devoted to each other, and after so many years."

"Joan mentioned her ex-son-in-law," Angie said.

"Dave Belting," Francine said. "He and Joan's daughter weren't married very long. I think they were high school sweethearts. When they got a little older, they realized they weren't a good match. Joan told me the breakup was amicable, with no hard feelings on either side."

"That's what she told me, too," Angie said. "She also mentioned that she and Eugene ran into Dave when they were out shopping. His live-in girlfriend left him."

"Oh, gee, that's too bad. Her name is Lila Melanson. I know her cousin."

"Do you know Dave Belting?" Jenna asked.

"His mother owns an auto supply business. I've met her at business conferences. Dave was at a few of them. He's quiet, almost sort of shy. He seems to lack confidence."

"He manages his job at the company well?" Jenna questioned.

"I think so," Francine said. "Dave is a salesman there. He's supposed to be smart as a whip. I wondered why he remained in sales and hadn't moved up in the company. Maybe he isn't that ambitious. Maybe he's happy with what's he doing."

"Do you know any more about Dave?" Jenna set her mug on the counter.

Francine's eyebrows knitted together as she thought about Dave Belting. "I think Dave went to Yale. I could be wrong about that, but that's what I think I heard. Didn't Joan and Eugene's daughter go to Yale, too?"

Angie and Jenna shrugged.

"Joan told me Dave and her daughter went to the same college, but she didn't say where they went," Angie said.

"I don't think I know anything else about Dave," Francine said. "Why do you ask about him?"

We were just thinking about people who might fit the profile of an arsonist," Jenna said.

"The arsonist?" Francine's vice was almost shrill. "You think the arsonist is someone we know?"

"It's a possibility," Angie said.

"What's the profile of an arsonist?"

Angie explained what they'd learned from Chief Martin.

"But Dave doesn't fit the age of the usual arsonist," Francine said. "He's in his thirties."

"There are exceptions to every situation," Jenna pointed out.

"Did your friend, Marine, ever tell you that Noah had an interest in fires?" Angie asked.

"She only said that he wanted to be a firefighter." Francine's eyes widened and her mouth dropped open a little. "Oh, no. Noah? Has he been setting the fires?"

"We're only speculating wildly about people," Angie said in a calm voice. "We don't know anything. We're not accusing anyone."

"Noah fits some of the profile, doesn't he?" Francine said. "He doesn't get along with his parents. He's smart, but doesn't reach his potential. He fits the age-range, too."

Jenna asked, "Did Marine ever speak about Noah having a drinking or drug problem?"

"Marine said Noah drank and that he probably took some drugs, but she didn't talk about it like it was a problem."

"What about Dave? Do you know if he uses alcohol or drugs?" Jenna questioned.

"I don't know," Francine said, and then her tone sounded indignant. "Wouldn't it be unbelievable if that arsonist has been under our noses all this time and we didn't even consider him to be the one who has been making all the trouble? All those buildings burned. Two people dead. And we might actually know the arsonist? I hope not. It would just be too much."

After leaving Francine's shop, Jenna and Angie headed back to the Victorian.

"Do you think the arsonist is a member of the Silver Cove community?" Jenna asked her sister.

"Yes, I do."

"So do I. What should we do next?"

"Let's see if Francine can organize that girls' night out. She's going to invite her cousin and ask her to bring Lila, Dave's ex-girlfriend. Let's hope she can arrange it. Maybe we can have a talk with Lila to hear about Dave," Angie suggested.

"What about Noah?"

"That's a tough one. What if the arsonist is the son of a Silver Cove police officer?"

"It would be bad if the arsonist has been right

under his father's nose and the father hasn't recognized what's happening," Jenna said.

Angie eyed her twin sister. "It would be even worse if the father knows what's going on and hasn't done anything about it."

16

Francine invited ten women to meet for drinks and appetizers at the Sweet Cove resort. Among the women who came was Francine's cousin who brought along Lila Melanson. Sitting in the lounge at tables in front of the fireplace, everyone chatted and enjoyed the food and drink.

"This was a great idea," one of the women announced. "I haven't been out like this for ages."

Most of the friends and acquaintances were women who owned their own businesses so there was plenty to talk about and share between them.

After an hour passed, Angie moved to a small group that included Lila. She introduced herself and asked how Lila knew Francine.

"I really don't know her. I'm a friend of Francine's cousin." Lila had chin-length light brown hair and blue eyes. In her thirties, she was slim but curvy, friendly and attractive.

"What do you do?" Angie asked.

"I'm an accountant. I have my own business," Lila said.

Angie told the woman about her bake shop and about her sisters and what they did for work.

"Really? That's your sister who runs the candy store? I love that place."

After talking for fifteen minutes, Lila revealed that she'd recently broken up with her boyfriend and moved out of the apartment.

"How long were you together?" Angie asked.

"Too long. A little over two years. I knew after a year that it wouldn't work out, but it was like inertia set in and I couldn't muster the energy to break it off." Lila frowned.

"What was wrong with the relationship?"

Lila forced a chuckle. "Everything. Dave was smart, but he didn't have any drive. I could never figure out if he lacked confidence or if he lacked initiative. He worked for his mother's company. I felt like it might have been better if he worked some- where else. He seemed too tied to his mother. The job was too easy for him. I tried to bring it up, but he would shut down the conversation."

Angie said, "I think I met Dave's ex-in-laws. The Fosters. I think he was married to one of their daughters."

"That's right. Lorrie Foster was Dave's first wife. They weren't married long."

"Did Dave ever marry after he and Lorrie divorced?"

"No, that was his only marriage," Lila said. "I bet he'll never get married again."

"Why do you say that?"

"Dave is under his mother's thumb. He's too much of a mama's boy."

"How did the two of you meet?"

"At some business gathering. I don't even remember what it was." Lila pushed her bangs to the side and let out a sigh. "You know, sometimes I miss Dave. He had a good heart. He was nice to me. He was just so weak-willed that it drove me nuts. I do think he recognizes his weakness. Sometimes, he drinks too much, and then he gets really sad. I think he feels trapped and he can't escape his mother's meddling. She is always telling him what to do. Forget it if I had a different opinion or idea. It wouldn't be considered. He followed his mother's instructions to the letter."

"Did you ever see Dave lose his temper?" Angie asked.

Lila looked surprised. "No, never. He might get slightly annoyed now and then, or mildly angry, but he never lost control of his emotions. That isn't Dave. He would never do that."

Angie was about to ask something else when Lila said, "Dave is very upset about the arsonist. When the first fire happened, he suggested we move to another town. He didn't think it was safe. I told him maybe we should look around. Dave mentioned to his mother that he was thinking of moving and she shot him down, basically said he had to stay in Silver Cove to be close to the business. Dave backed down. That was really the last straw for me. I can't live with someone so weak-willed. I just can't."

Angie and Lila talked some more about the fires.

Lila said, "I was in the center of Silver Cove on the night the business building was set on fire. I was out to dinner with a friend. I know the accountant whose office burned up in the fire. He's devastated. He's planning to leave the state."

"That's terrible. Do you think he'll reconsider?"

"I don't." Lila took a swallow from her glass of

wine. "My friend and I went outside to watch the fire that night. I've never seen anything like it. The heat coming off the fire was unbelievable. My friend left and I was about to go to my car. I saw this guy off in the distance. His face looked so ... I don't know how to describe it. He looked thrilled by the fire. It made me feel weird."

Angie's heart started to pound. "What did he look like?"

"Sort of an average guy. Slim, dressed in business casual clothes. Black hair, worn a little longer. He had a beard. He wore glasses. He really wouldn't stand out to anyone, except his eyes were wacky. It was like he was delighted by the fire, mesmerized. There was some strange energy coming off of him. I even wondered if he was the arsonist."

"Where were you standing?"

Lila told her. It wasn't far from where Angie and Jenna had been standing when they saw the guy who made Angie feel uneasy.

Lila shuddered. "He really gave me the creeps."

"Would you recognize him if you saw him again?"

"Probably not. That's how average he was. But if a fire was blazing and he was there, I bet I'd recognize him because he'd look kind of crazed."

"How old would you say he was?"

"Mid-to-late twenties?"

Angie felt her blood go cold. The man Lila was describing sounded similar to the guy who had made her anxious at the fire scene.

"Had you ever seen him before?"

"No. At least I don't think so."

When some women came over to join Angie and Lila, Angie wandered away to go sit next to Jenna.

Keeping her voice down, she told her sister, "Lila saw a man whose behavior was similar to the one who made me so anxious at the fire. She described his expression the way I remember him. She said his eyes were wacky, like he was delighted by the blaze."

"Did she see where he went?"

"No, she wanted to get away from him. She didn't bother to watch where he went."

"This could be the same man that the salesclerk saw that night," Jenna said.

"I'd bet money on it."

"Did Lila say how old the man seemed to be?"

"Mid-to-late twenties."

"Who is this guy?" Jenna asked.

"By the way, Dave Belting needs to be removed from the suspect list. Lila describes him as a mama's boy. She said he was upset about the fires. It doesn't seem like he could be the arsonist."

Jenna sat quietly for a few moments. "An overbearing mother? That's part of an arsonist's profile."

"But Dave was upset about the fires, about the damage that was done."

"Was he? Maybe that's a reaction he has *after* he sets a fire. Or maybe it's a front he puts on to trick people, to make it seem impossible that he could be the firebug."

"Oh, gee. I was ready to dismiss him."

"I think that's premature," Jenna said. "We also need to find out more about Noah Pandy."

"His age matches up with the profile of an arsonist," Angie pointed out. "He's in his twenties."

"There are other characteristics Noah shares with an arsonist," Jenna said. "He doesn't get along with his parents. He's smart, but underachieves. He can't keep a job."

"An accelerant was used in the latest fire," Angie said. "It was put inside a beer bottle."

"A not so common brand of beer," Jenna said. "And one that happened to be Noah's dad's favorite beer."

"What does Noah look like?" Angie asked. "Is he average looking? Slim? Brown hair?"

"Do his eyes look wacky when he's watching a fire?" Jenna questioned.

"Is Noah the man the salesclerk and Lila saw at the fire?"

Jenna narrowed her eyes and let out a sigh. "I think it's time to find out a little more about Noah Pandy."

17

Wearing her wedding gown, Angie stood in front of the full-length mirror in Ellie's room as her sister knelt on the floor with pins in her mouth adjusting the hem.

Euclid and Circe sat on the bed supervising the activity.

When Angie ran her hands over the white fabric of the skirt, Ellie chided her. "Don't look down. You'll mess up the length. It will be shorter in some places if you don't keep your head up."

Angie looked at her image in the mirror. Wearing her mother's wedding dress made her feel closer to her mom. It was almost as if she was right in the next room about to come in to give Angie a loving hug and help Ellie hem the flowing gown. Sometimes she forgot how much she missed her mother.

Blinking back a few tears, Angie cleared her throat. "Why doesn't Jenna ever see Mom's spirit? Why doesn't Mom come to see us?"

Surprised, Ellie looked up at her sister and took the pins from between her lips. "I don't know. Maybe she does come to see us, but we just can't see her."

"If she was here, why wouldn't Jenna be able to see her?"

Ellie sat back on her butt. "Did you ask Jenna? She's the one who can see ghosts. I don't understand any of these *skills*. The whole thing is baffling to me." A little smile played across Ellie's lips. "And we all know how I feel about things I can't understand."

Ellie needed to have an understanding of the things she was involved in … doing taxes, incorporating her business, what a job would entail, how much interest would she have to pay on a loan. If she didn't have a full understanding of what she was getting into, then she preferred not to do it or take it on. Paranormal abilities were way outside of her comfort zone.

Angie smiled. "You and Mom were always a lot alike, intelligent, careful, deliberate … you both always need to understand what's going on and how it will impact the family. You're even the daughter who looks most like her."

Ellie tilted her head to the side. "I see a lot of Mom in your face, especially when you have her gown on."

Euclid trilled at the comment.

"I wish she was here," Angie whispered and batted at her eyes.

"We miss Mom the most at times like these," Ellie said. "Holidays, birthdays, weddings, when something good happens and we want to tell her, or when something bad happens and we want her comfort."

Circe jumped down from the bed and rubbed her head against Angie's leg covered with the soft, white material. The cat looked up at Angie with loving green eyes and purred softly.

"Sweet cat." Angie bent to pat the feline. "Always makes me feel better."

Ellie took in a long breath. "Okay, stand straight and let's get this hemming done."

When Angie moved her shoulders back to stand tall, she thought she saw movement behind her reflected in the mirror. For a half-second, she thought she saw her mother standing right behind her.

WHEN THE DRESS fitting was done, Angie and Ellie decided to go to town for a bite to eat and strolled the brick sidewalks through the center to the Pirate's Den restaurant where they were seated at a table near the windows. The lunch rush was over and it was a little too early for the dinner crowd, so the sisters had the place almost to themselves.

"Haven't seen you two for a couple of weeks." Bessie Lindquist, a small, petite woman with delicate features and short silvery-blond hair that framed her high cheekbones, smiled broadly as she set down the menus. Bessie and her husband had owned the Pirate's Den for over twenty years. "Good timing. The lunch crowd just cleared out. A lull before the next storm." The energetic woman let out a laugh. "The wedding is getting real close now," she said to Angie. "Everything all set?"

"Pretty much," Angie said.

Ellie shook her head. "Miss Last Minute has everything under control."

Bessie said, "We all work at our own pace and in our own way. It all gets done."

A waiter came by and took drink orders and then the conversation turned to town news.

"I hear you're going to interview for the open seat on the finance board," Bessie said to Ellie.

"I am. I've been working hard to prepare."

"When's the interview?"

"In a few days."

"You'd better be the one they choose. You're a fabulous business person and you're good with numbers and at understanding the needs of the town and the people. When your appointed term is up and you run for reelection, not only will I vote for you, but I'll campaign for you as well."

"Thank you so much." Ellie was stunned at Bessie's praise.

Bessie smiled. "I've been talking you up to town officials, too."

With a chuckle, Ellie said, "I need to make you my campaign manager."

"Good luck with the interview, but you aren't going to need it." Bessie turned the conversation to the Silver Cove fires. "Terrible, someone terrorizing the town. My sister lives there. Luckily, her neighborhood hasn't been hit by this fire nut, but she's only a few blocks from where he set three of the fires. We all hope the person is caught before he can do any more damage or take any more lives."

The waiter brought the drinks to the table, took the orders, and went to enter them in at the computer.

Bessie sat down with the sisters and spoke in a soft tone. "We've been afraid the arsonist will head down this way and start setting fires in Sweet Cove. We hired a security guard to watch the restaurant when it's closed. It's expensive, but not as expensive as losing all of the business if we got hit, not to mention having to rebuild or renovate."

"The whole thing is a big mess." Ellie lifted her glass to her lips. "I think you're smart to protect your business."

"Like everyone else, we really hope the person is caught soon." Bessie folded her hands in her lap. "I'd be a nervous wreck if we were located in Silver Cove. I'm a nervous wreck anyway worrying about my sister. Why on earth would someone set fires?"

The chat moved away from the Silver Cove troubles and to the difficulty finding seasonal workers. "This year has been the hardest. Next month, the tourist season pushes into high gear and we still don't have all the staff we need. There are fewer workers applying from other countries and the people we hire from here often don't work out. I would love to staff the openings with people from the area, but there just aren't enough workers who apply. We even bumped up the wages."

"Do you get some people who want to only work part time?" Angie asked.

"Oh, sure, and we love to hire them. We can manage just fine with a bunch of part time workers." Bessie checked over her shoulders. "The two from town I hired this month didn't work out. I had to let them go. No work ethic. I hired one of them as a favor to a police officer in Silver Cove."

Angie's interest piqued. "Really? Why do you say *as a favor* since you need workers so badly?"

Bessie said, "The young man had no references. He has a poor work history. He was asked to leave college for a while because he wasn't going to classes or doing the work. I was happy to give him a chance. Unfortunately, I couldn't keep him."

"What happened?" Angie knew full well who Bessie was probably talking about. It had to be Noah Pandy.

"He never showed up for his shifts on time. Sometimes, he came in an hour after he was supposed to be here. Once, he didn't show up at all and when he came in for his next shift, he said he'd been sick. I told him he had to call the restaurant to tell us if he wasn't able to come in. He just blew me off."

Bessie shook her head. "We'd assign him tasks and he'd do them in a half-baked way. We had to keep him in the kitchen, no way he could interact with customers. One night, we were so busy and I found him outside the back door listening to music on his phone and smoking. He didn't care. He was standing there flicking his lighter off and on, staring at the flame. He didn't care one bit about what I was saying to him."

"Really?" Ellie said. "Did you fire him then?"

"I felt terrible about it. His family is trying so hard to get him on track, but we had to let the young man go," Bessie said. "We gave him every possible chance and I hated to give up on him, but he just blew it."

"That's too bad," Ellie said. "Maybe he needs to fail a bunch of times in order to pick himself up."

Angie leaned forward. "Was it Noah Pandy?"

Bessie blinked fast several times. "How did you know? Do you know the family?"

"I've met his father," Angie told her. "I heard the son was sort of difficult."

"I feel bad for his mom and dad. I don't know what they can do to turn him around. I think they're trying to think of everything they can." Bessie bit her lower lip. "The way he was staring at the flame on his lighter sort of freaked me out. It made me wonder." The woman glanced around the restaurant. "I wondered if he could be the one who's been setting the fires."

The three sat in silence thinking about Noah Pandy.

"You know, the night the Willoughby's house was set on fire, I was visiting my sister in Silver Cove. A friend called her to tell her about the fire. We decided to walk over there to see what was happening. I swear I saw Noah hurrying away from the neighborhood."

18

Sitting on the sofa in the family room in her pajamas with Euclid on one side of her and Circe on the other, Angie spooned some ice cream into her mouth. She dipped her finger into the bowl and offered the cats a lick which they gratefully accepted. Their rough little tongues moved over the finger working at picking up every last drop of the vanilla goodness.

Just as she reached for the television remote, the doorbell rang causing Angie to sigh. No one else was at home so she would have to walk out to the foyer to open the door. The cats ran ahead and were waiting at the door before Angie got there.

The fur on Euclid's back was sticking up.

"What's wrong, Euclid?" Angie hesitated to open the door.

The bell rang again and her heart began to race.

"Who's there?"

"It's me." Chief Martin's voice spoke from behind the door. Angie swung it open.

"The cats were acting weird. I'm alone. I was nervous about opening the door."

"It's only me, but maybe the cats are picking up on what's going on in Silver Cove." The chief's face was drawn with concern. "Two more fires. Going on right now."

"Two?" Angie groaned.

"Can you come with me or do you need to stay here?"

"I can come," she said, even though she really didn't want to go. She was feeling rundown like she was getting a cold, and she'd been feeling helpless and hopeless about catching the arsonist. "I'll run upstairs to change."

In the squad car, the chief shared what he knew. "I just got the call. A building on Main Street is engulfed. It's a four-story business building. The second fire is in a neighborhood, a ranch house."

Angie's heart skipped a beat. "What neighborhood?" She held her breath hoping it wasn't Joan's and Eugene's house.

"It's on the north side of the town."

Angie blew out a breath of relief that the Fosters had been spared. She worried about the older couple. Their health wasn't great and they didn't move quickly. If a fire started in their house, would they be able to get out in time?

"Which one are we going to?" Angie asked.

"I thought I'd drop you off on Main Street. The Silver Cove officers asked if I'd head up to the fire on the other side of town because most of the force is at the Main Street fire. They need some help at the other one. My thinking is that you might see something when you're on Main Street. It's a bigger fire. If the arsonist was going to stay at one of them, I'm guessing he'd choose that one. More people to mingle in with. More excitement to fuel his need for importance."

"That's fine." Angie rubbed at her temple. Her head and neck felt tight and a few little pinprick-sized flashes danced in her vision. *Not a migraine. Not now.*

The chief pulled to the curb and Angie got out. Through the open window, Chief Martin said to her, "Be careful. Stay with the crowd. Officer Pandy is

here somewhere. Look for him if you need anything.
Thanks, Angie. Keep in touch."

Angie saw the crowds gathered in groups on the
opposite side of the four-story inferno. Powerful
streams of water were being directed at the building.
Fire engines and police cars parked in the middle of
the street and officials darted back and forth among
the personnel.

The rotating blue lights on top of the police cars
burned her eyes and she had to look away. A slight
pulsing had started in her forehead.

Moving away from the spot where the chief
dropped her off, she made her way down the sidewalk to the first group of people.

"Did everyone get out?" she asked no one in
particular.

"Lots of people got out," a young woman told
her. "But there might be others still in there. No one
is sure."

Angie shuddered thinking about people who
might be trapped in the burning building. A
terrible stink of burning materials filled the air
and almost made her gag. Smoke billowed up
into the night sky in huge undulating black
waves.

Feeling heavy and lacking in energy, she made

her way further into the crowd, listening to people's comments and searching their faces.

"When will the police catch this guy," someone said in an angry tone. "How hard could it be?"

Angie rolled her eyes and thought, *Harder than anything you've probably had to do.*

"It scares me," a woman told the person next to her. "It's happening more frequently. There are two fires going at once tonight."

The woman's friend said, "It's all escalating. It won't be long before he sets three fires at once. It makes me want to move away, get out of here before I'm one of the victims."

Angie heard similar things as she moved through the throngs of people. Fear. Anger. Impatience with the police progress. Occasionally, she'd pass by a couple of young men saying inappropriate things about how exciting it was to finally have something going on in town.

One rough-looking guy said something insensitive about the men and women who might be trapped in the building. Angie glared at the idiot wishing she could punch him in the nose.

With her headache worsening, Angie ducked into a convenience store for an ice cold bottle of water. She held the bottle to her forehead and then against both temples trying to stave off the worst of the pain. If it wasn't for the fire, she'd grab a cab and head straight home, but she needed to stay and look around. She didn't want to let Chief Martin down.

Continuing her way along the sidewalk, Angie moved past more gawkers and each step she took made it feel like a vise was tightening around her head. She stepped to the back of the crowd and leaned against a brick building trying to collect herself while keeping an eye and ear on the proceedings.

Someone in the group directly ahead of her caught her attention.

A young man with brown hair, dressed in chinos and a collared, button down shirt, stood next to three men and two women, but none of them seemed to know one another. They all had their gazes pinned to the blazing building. Every few minutes, one of them would make a comment about the fire. When the young man angled his body so he could see better, Angie was able to see the wide grin he had plastered on his face.

Was this the man she noticed the other night? The one who had made her feel so uneasy.

Steadying herself, Angie moved closer until she was right behind the young man. She tried to clear her head so that she might be able to pick up on whatever emotions the man was giving off.

All she could sense was a bit of excitement, but also more of an interest in how the firefighters were attempting to subdue the fire.

She turned away quickly and started for the next group when she collided with someone hurrying up the sidewalk. The crash, combined with the headache, almost made her topple and she closed her eyes for a moment.

"Look at that fire. It's pretty amazing," a man's voice said.

Angie's eyelids flashed open.

"Have you been watching? It went up like a dry piece of tinder. Look at the flames. Look how high they're shooting into the air." The man's eyes looked wild.

Angie's stomach clenched and she had to take deep breaths to keep the head pain from making her sway. The man didn't even notice her distress.

She judged the young man standing in front of her to be in his twenties or thirties. He had longer brown hair, cut at an angle. The sides didn't quite make it to his chin. He wore black-rimmed eyeglasses and had a brown mustache. He wore a collared, long-sleeved shirt and expensive-looking slacks. She could smell alcohol on his breath.

"Have you been watching long?" the man asked Angie.

When Angie shook her head, it felt like pieces of glass were shifting around in her brain.

She couldn't help but stare at the man next to her. The headache made her vision blur and she couldn't clearly see the man's features.

Something was off, but she couldn't make out what it was. The heavy smell of the alcohol made Angie's stomach lurch. She took a step back.

The man turned his face to the fire and Angie could see his breathing rate increase. Whatever seeped from the guy's pores made Angie want to wretch. Anxiety pulsed through her veins. Perspiration formed on her brow as the pain in her forehead increased. She tried to say something to the man, but the words wouldn't come out.

"It's beautiful, isn't it?" the man said with wonder in his voice.

When Angie reached out to touch the man's arm to get his attention, her fingers felt like they'd touched hot coals and she yanked her hand back.

The man stared at her for one full moment. "I need to go." He pulled some keys from his back pocket and walked to the car parked on the corner. He unlocked the door and got in. The engine started.

Angie wanted to run after him. She couldn't let him get away. Her feet wouldn't move. She could not budge from her spot on the sidewalk.

Take a photo of the car.

Angie forced her hand to fumble around inside her purse trying to grab onto her phone.

The vehicle moved away from its parked position.

Angie couldn't get the phone out in time.

The license plate. Look at the license plate.

The migraine made the car's license plate numbers wiggle and shimmer and shrink in her vision.

Squint. Remember the numbers, Angie ordered her brain.

The car pulled away and was gone.

That was him. That was him.

Angie backed up towards the building behind her, pushed her back against the bricks, and slid slowly down to the sidewalk. She pulled her knees to her chest and rested her head against them ... and used all of her power not to vomit.

19

Angie sat on the family room sofa with her sunglasses on and an ice pack on her head. Her sisters, Mr. Finch, and the cats had seats on the other chairs and sofa in the room and each one took turns fussing over the young woman.

From her position sitting on the sidewalk in Silver Cove, Angie was able to place a call to Ellie and the whole family arrived in the van to rescue her from the migraine. Even the cats came along and sat close to Angie on the van's bench seat as they all made the drive home together.

Back at the Victorian, they hustled Angie into the house, gave her some medication and brought her a cup of tea. Mr. Finch knew that the migraine made Angie's eyes light-sensitive so he found her sunglasses and had her put them on. Courtney got an ice pack and wrapped it in a light towel so Angie could hold it to her head.

Euclid squashed himself next to her on the sofa and when Jenna brought her sister a soft blanket to put over her lap, the big orange cat burrowed under it.

Circe curled up on the young woman's lap and Angie ran her hand over the silky ebony fur.

"I'm starting to feel better," Angie announced, her voice still weak.

Ellie darted to the kitchen and a few minutes later carried in a plate of buttered toast with a little jam. Angie thanked everyone for their help and began to nibble on the toast.

Courtney chuckled at how her sister looked sitting with toast in her hand, a cat on her lap, an ice pack on her head, and her sunglasses on. "I'm going to take your picture and post it on social media ... or if you'd rather, you can use it as your engagement photo. You look like some washed-up young starlet."

"Thanks a lot," Angie muttered.

"Since you're now able to talk, sis, why don't you tell us what happened in Silver Cove?" Courtney asked.

"Perhaps, Miss Angie needs a bit more time to rest," Mr. Finch suggested.

"She can rest after she tells us what went on up there," Courtney smiled.

"Are you up to it?" Jenna asked.

Angie attempted a nod, but grimaced when she moved her head. "As long as I sit perfectly still, I think I can talk."

"Stop if you have to rest," Ellie said.

Angie told them that Chief Martin came by and said there were two fires in Silver Cove. He asked her to go along and he dropped her off on Main Street while he went to the second fire.

"My head started to pound. I knew a migraine was coming on, but I hoped I could look around for a while before it really kicked in."

"What did you see?" Jenna asked.

"Crowds had gathered in groups on the sidewalk. The fire was in full force. The fire shot high into the air." Angie adjusted her ice pack. "I walked through the groups of people listening to what they were saying. I was looking for anyone who seemed suspicious."

"And? Did you see anyone?" Courtney leaned forward with a hopeful expression on her face.

"I started to feel really ill. My eyes hurt, my

vision was weird, images started to swim and shimmer. It felt like I was outside of my body, that everything around me was happening in a dream."

"Did something happen?" Mr. Finch asked.

"I bumped into a young man. Maybe he was in his twenties or a little older. He smelled like alcohol, a lot of alcohol."

"Did he speak to you?" Ellie fiddled nervously with a long strand of her hair.

Angie was about to nod, but stopped herself before making the move she knew would cause her head to hurt. "Yes, he did. He was gawking at the fire. He said it was beautiful."

Jenna's eyebrow went up and Euclid hissed from under the blanket.

"He asked if I'd seen the building go up in flames. He was impressed at how high the blaze shot into the sky," Angie said. "Other people were saying similar things, but this guy had a strange sense of excitement and amazement in his voice. It didn't seem ... normal."

"Then what happened?" Courtney asked.

"The man said other things in the same vein." Angie rubbed her head. "Something about him made me feel worse, like I was going to pass out. It wasn't just the migraine. There was something wrong with this man. He took too much delight in the fire."

"Did you say anything to him?" Ellie asked.

"I tried to ask him something, but I couldn't get the words out of my throat. I think I reached out and touched his arm." Angie paused for a few seconds. "Yes, yes, I did. I touched his arm. When I touched him, my fingers felt like they'd touched fire."

"Oh," Ellie gasped and her hand flew to the side of her face. "It *was* him."

Everyone, except Angie, turned to look at the blond sitting in the white club chair.

"You mean the arsonist?" Jenna kept her tone even.

"It was him, wasn't it, Angie?" Ellie asked with wide eyes.

"It was." The words could barely be heard when Angie whispered them. "It was him. I touched him." She rubbed her fingers over the blanket as if she were trying to remove something bad from her hand.

"Are you able to describe him, Miss Angie?" Finch asked kindly.

"He was average height, slender. He had brown hair and wore it slightly longer than most men his age. He had a mustache. The man was dressed in nice-looking slacks and a long sleeve shirt. Oh, he wore eyeglasses, sort of the same shape and style as Mr. Finch's glasses."

"Black rims?" Courtney asked.

"Yes. They were black."

"Like the monster's heart," Ellie said with disgust.

"Did he have any distinguishing features?" Jenna questioned her sister. "A tattoo? A scar? A bent nose? Big ears?"

"His face was bland. Nothing stood out. My vision was terrible, everything looked odd," Angie said. "I might have missed something important about him. I did the best I could."

"You sure did," Courtney praised her. "Someone else would have given up if they were in the throes of a migraine."

"Did the man walk away?" Finch watched Angie's face.

"He did." Angie's voice was getting weaker.

"Did you see where he went?" Jenna asked.

"Yes. He went to his car."

"You saw his car?" Courtney leapt to her feet. "You saw him get into a car?"

"Yes." Angie sighed. "I know what you're going to ask next."

"You're right about the next question ... and I'll ask it," Courtney told her. "What kind of car was it?"

"I'm not quite sure."

Courtney let out a loud groan.

Angie defended herself. "I was about to pass out. Nothing seemed real. I knew I needed to look at the car, but it was so hard to do. I tried to focus, but it made me feel sicker."

"So you don't know anything about the car?" Jenna asked.

"It was dark, maybe dark blue. Not black though. It had four doors. It was sort of plain. It didn't look old. It seemed to be in good condition."

"Yes!" Courtney high-fived Mr. Finch. "Nice work, sis. Chief Martin is going to love this."

"Should I call him?" Jenna asked. "Report to him what you saw?"

"Hold up a second." Angie leaned her head slowly onto the back of the sofa.

"Do you need to rest?" Ellie asked.

"No. I need to think for a minute."

Euclid stuck his head out from under the blanket and stared at Angie.

"What do you need to think about?" Courtney moved to sit on the floor in front of her sister.

"The license plate," Angie said softly.

"You saw the license plate?" Courtney nearly howled causing Angie to wince.

"Not so loud, please," Angie requested.

"Sorry." Courtney lowered her voice, but couldn't keep her excitement out of her tone. "You saw the license plate?"

"Part of it."

"What state was it from?" Mr. Finch asked the easiest question first.

"Massachusetts," Angie said.

The family members exchanged looks with one another.

"Did you see any of the numbers on the plate?" Ellie asked, afraid she would hear an answer in the negative.

Angie didn't respond right away. She was trying to pull some numbers from her memory, but they weren't cooperating.

Jenna went to sit next to her twin. "Anything? Did you see anything at all?"

Ellie sat with a notebook in her lap and a pen held at the ready.

"5 ... B ... there was an 8, too, but it wasn't in order. Those are the numbers and the letter I saw. I just can't recall what order they were in," Angie said.

"That's great, that's really great, sis," Courtney

said. "That's amazing. *You're* amazing. We're so proud of you. Can Jenna call Chief Martin now and tell him this stuff?"

"Yes."

"Are you feeling okay, Miss Angie?" Finch asked in a caring tone of voice.

"I'm okay." Angie still had her eyes closed. "I'm really hungry all of a sudden."

"What would you like?" Ellie asked.

"I'd love a fried egg. Would someone be able to make me one?"

"Two fried eggs coming right up." Finch grabbed his cane and started for the kitchen. "A little cheese sprinkled over the top?"

"Oh, yes, please." Angie's mouth started to water at the thought of the eggs. "I'd also eat a banana, if we have any left."

Euclid jumped onto the floor and Circe leapt down to chase after him as the two felines flew into the hallway to run for the kitchen.

"One banana, coming right up," Finch announced as he was about to leave the room. "Anything for our hero, Angie Roseland."

20

Sitting next to Angie on the sofa, Jenna tapped at her laptop to do an internet search.

"What are you doing?" Angie asked.

"None of us know what Dave Belting or Noah Pandy look like. I want to see if there are any photos of them on the internet, maybe on social media. We can compare them to the description you gave us of the arsonist."

"We can't be sure the man I saw is the arsonist," Angie said.

"Yes, we can." Jenna leaned slightly closer to better see the screen. "Look." She took a glance at her sister. "Can you look or are your eyes still bothering you?"

Angie moved her sunglasses up a little. "If I can wear my sunglasses while I look, it might be okay."

Jenna slid the laptop onto her sister's lap and pointed. "See this guy? Does he look familiar?"

Angie sat quietly for a few seconds. "You said the word familiar. It made me think of something. The guy I saw tonight ... he almost seemed a little familiar to me."

"Really? Can you think of where you might have seen him?"

"I don't know. I can't match him to a place. Still, I think I might have seen him before. Maybe."

"Did he look like this man?" Jenna lifted the laptop so Angie wouldn't have to lean down.

"There are similarities," Angie said. "It could be the same person, but it might not be."

Jenna tapped some more. "How about this one? What do you think about him?"

"Again, there are similarities. It's hard to say. Maybe that picture isn't up-to-date."

"These men are definite possibilities? Neither is a definite *no*?"

"Their coloring is the same as the man I ran into. Body shape and size look the same," Angie said. "I wouldn't rule them out, but I can't say for certain that one of these men is the same guy I saw this evening."

"This one is Dave Belting. And this one is Noah Pandy." Jenna tipped the laptop to eliminate the glare.

"Something about the man this evening seemed familiar," Angie mentioned again. "But something seemed off when I looked at him."

"It must have been the effects of the migraine on your vision," Jenna suggested.

"I don't know. It seemed like more than that," Angie said. "But I don't know what or why."

"Maybe it will come to you later when you've eaten and rested," Jenna said. "Let your brain rest for now."

"Look who I found on our front porch." Courtney led Chief Martin into the family room.

"Sorry to hear you're feeling poorly, Angie," the chief said in a softer than usual voice. "I understand you got some good information this evening."

"Pardon my appearance," Angie kidded. "I'm not looking my best."

"No worries," the chief said. "You've seen me at my worst." Chief Martin was referring to being attacked by a criminal and injected with an opioid that almost killed him. If not for Angie's fast thinking and quick action, the chief would have died that day.

The chief took a seat and happily accepted the mug of coffee Courtney brought to him.

"Mr. Finch is making Angie a fried egg," Courtney told the chief. "Would you like some?"

"If it's not too much trouble, I'd love a fried egg. I haven't eaten for hours."

"How was the second fire?" Angie asked. "No one was hurt, were they?"

"Everyone was safe," the chief nodded. "The house is a shambles. I don't think it can be salvaged."

"Too bad. The poor family." Angie took the ice pack from her head and placed it on the coffee table on a place mat.

"Some people in Silver Cove have started a fund for the victims," the chief said. "To help with the financial side of the trouble."

"That's very kind of them."

"How's your head?" he asked.

"Like it got hit by a sledgehammer," Angie said. "Twice."

"You want to wait until tomorrow to talk?"

"No, I'll be okay."

"Good. It's better for me to get the information as soon as possible. If you've retold the story a bunch of times, it runs the risk of becoming distorted. Things change in the retelling. I guess it's human nature." The chief took a long swallow of the hot coffee. "That's good. I needed that," he said as he set down the mug. "Are you able to tell me what went on?"

Angie responded positively and retold the narrative of the evening. "I watched him get into the car. I tried to memorize the license plate, but the headache kept me from remembering much."

The chief repeated the numbers and the letter he was told when Jenna called him with the news. "Are those the numbers and letter you saw on the plate?"

"Yes. I hope I can remember more once I've been able to sleep."

The rest of the family came into the room and settled in their seats as Finch and Ellie presented plates of food to Angie and the chief.

"Thanks for the eggs. Delicious." Chief Martin cleared his throat and looked at Angie. "Have you ever been hypnotized?"

"What? Why?"

"We could have a professional hypnotist work with you to see if you can recall anything else," the chief said. "The method can help a person access the information in their brain that they think they don't know."

"Really?" Courtney asked. "That's so cool. I'd do it."

"I don't know," Angie thought about what the chief proposed. "It works?"

"We've used hypnosis several times in cases to bring out all the details a person knows, but is unable to get at," Chief Martin explained. "You most likely saw the entire license plate, but the storage of the information might be disorganized. The forensic hypnotist can help you with that."

"It couldn't hurt Miss Angie, could it?" Finch asked the chief.

"Not at all. You either get some more information or you don't. No harm is done to the subject," the chief said.

"I guess I could give it a try," Angie said.

"We can make arrangements to see the hypnotist later in the week," the chief said. "The investigator found something interesting at the second fire."

"What is it?" Jenna asked the question everyone in the room was eager to hear.

"Another craft beer bottle. High Stars. It was used to hold the accelerant."

"That brand again," Angie said.

"It may prove to be a valuable clue," the chief said.

"Officer Pandy said that particular beer was his favorite," Angie said. "Maybe he doesn't realize what he's actually saying. That his appreciation of fine beers could drag him into this case, and not as an officer of the law, but as the father of an arsonist."

Chief Martin shook his head. "I hope not, but if that's where the path leads...."

"The man I saw tonight bears a resemblance to Noah," Angie said.

"If Officer Pandy thought his son was guilty of arson, why would he even admit that brand of beer was his favorite?" Jenna asked.

"I don't know," the chief said. "I don't think he considers his son a suspect. I've been thinking I might do some digging into the whereabouts of Noah Pandy on the evenings of the fires."

"What about Dave Belting?" Courtney asked. "The man Angie saw also looks like Belting. Shouldn't you try to determine where he was on the nights the fires were lit?"

"I'm on that one already." The chief gave a nod. "So far, we don't have any clear answers about where Belting was on the nights of the fires."

"Does he drink High Stars beer?" Ellie asked.

"No answer yet on that either," the chief said.

"Are there suspects other than Belting and Pandy?" Finch asked.

"There is one other person of interest."

"Have you managed to determine if this person drinks that brand of beer?" Jenna asked.

"Yes, he does." The chief shifted in his chair. "The three men we're considering are all long-shots for suspects. We really only have some vague speculation that any of these three men could be guilty. We have to take baby steps. We need to honor protocol. We can't step on toes. We need to tread carefully."

"Understandable," Ellie said.

"Who is the hypnotist you want me to see?" Angie questioned.

The chief said, "The man is from Boston, but will travel up here, if we request it. He's an older man, in his seventies. Still active. He works with police departments, with athletes, with professional people who have things that are holding them back in their work, like fear of presenting, fear of success, fear of flying. He's no kook. He's been the expert witness in court on many, many cases."

"It seems okay then." When Angie finished her eggs and leaned slowly forward to put her plate on the coffee table, she thanked Mr. Finch for making them for her, and then turned her gaze on the chief. "Will you tell us the name of the third possible suspect?"

Chief Martin ran his hand over his face. "I'd rather not."

"Why not?" Ellie asked.

"Because. It could be a little awkward."

Ellie sat ramrod straight. "You couldn't possibly be investigating one of us? Or one of our friends?"

"It's not any of you. Absolutely not."

Angie lifted the sunglasses so she could see from under the dark lenses. "Who is it then? We should know who a suspect is as we go about our business trying to find this arsonist in a haystack."

Chief Martin coughed. "What I tell you must stay between us and it cannot be repeated."

"We haven't betrayed your confidence yet," Courtney told him, and then tapped her chin with her index finger. "But there's always a first time."

"I'll ignore that comment," the chief said.

"Can you share the name of the person?" Finch asked.

Chief Martin shrugged. "The person's life is spinning out of control, what with family duties, work duties. It's possible that all the pressure may be pushing him over the edge, pushing him to commit these crimes."

Something flashed through Angie and she took a long look at the chief. "You're talking about Officer Pandy, aren't you?"

21

"A few of us are concerned about Officer Pandy." The chief's facial muscles had sagged with worry and sadness. "We hope he isn't the one who's been setting the fires, but he's been seen cruising around the neighborhoods and the Main Street area of town at odd hours. We'd be remiss if we didn't consider the possibility, much as it pains us to do so."

"But the man I saw didn't look like Officer Pandy," Angie had told the group.

"The headache played havoc with your vision. Your migraine might have messed up your ability to sense what was going on," Ellie spoke gently. "Maybe you were mistaken about the man you bumped into being the arsonist."

"I guess so." Angie wasn't ready to dismiss the man she ran into while at the fire as a suspect. Her feelings had been strong. She would have bet money on it. But ... the migraine *could* have interfered with her paranormal sensory abilities. Maybe the feedback she picked up on was actually wrong.

"What about having Angie work with a portrait artist, a forensic artist?" Courtney asked.

"What's that?" Ellie asked with a look of confusion.

"A facial composite artist," the chief explained. "A witness works with an artist who asks about a suspect's facial features, usually focusing on one feature at a time, the nose shape, the eyes, cheeks, and so on until a complete face has been drawn."

"What if the face I remember is wrong?" Angie asked. "What if my perception and my memory are incorrect because of the migraine?"

"It might be worth a shot to have you sit with an artist," Chief Martin said. "There is also the young woman who works as a salesclerk in Silver Cove. She ran into a man during the first fire on Main Street. Maybe it would be worthwhile to also have her sit with an artist to produce a face. Then the salesclerk's description can be compared with Angie's description. We can see if it's the same man."

Jenna said, "Angie and Anna Billings, the sales-clerk, both could smell alcohol on the man's breath. That's kind of unusual, isn't it? And the man said things about the fires that seemed inappropriate. It could very well be the same man that they ran into, and he could very well be the arsonist."

After a little more discussion, the family and Chief Martin dispersed and Angie dragged herself up the carved wooden staircase to her rooms where she showered and then crawled into bed and pulled the soft sheet up to her chin. The two fine felines accompanied Angie upstairs and settled on the bed to watch over her. The young woman's dreams steered clear of the fires and the arsonist, and instead, lulled her with sweet, comforting recollections of her mother.

ANGIE CLOSED the bake shop and headed to the Sweet Cove Police station. Her head still had lingering soreness and a bit of a foggy sensation that often followed a migraine. Anxiety pulsed in her blood, too. She was about to meet with the forensic artist who would complete a sketch of the suspect from the descriptions Angie provided.

An older gentleman greeted her warmly when she entered the conference room. "It's Angie, correct?" The man shook her hand, introduced himself, and gestured to a seat at the table next to where he would be sitting. "I've been doing this for a very long time. I'll ask some questions and show you some pictures of facial features. The pictures are here to help jog your brain. For example, it is easier to recognize a specific nose shape than to attempt to recall and describe it to me."

The man's manner and easy explanations reminded Angie of Mr. Finch and she immediately relaxed.

The artist asked Angie to describe the person she saw the other night.

She thought back to seeing the man and described the way he looked, starting with his eyes, moving to the shape of the forehead, the cheeks, lips, jawline, hair, and ears.

The artist made a faint preliminary sketch and then opened his manual to pages of noses ... big, little, some with a narrow bridge and some with very wide ones. A few noses had large nostrils, a few had small ones. There were long noses and tiny, short noses.

When they finished the nose, Angie and the

artist moved on to the eyes, and then covered the rest of the features including the mustache.

On completion, the man turned the sketchbook slightly so that Angie could better see the drawing.

A small gasp slipped from the young woman's throat when she looked into the eyes of the face on the paper. "Yes, it looks very much like him," she said softly. "The likeness is really amazing." Tilting her head to the side, she considered the picture for almost a full minute.

"Is there something you'd like to change?" the artist asked.

With her eyes narrowed, she said, "No. This is how the man looked."

"Do I hear a *but* in your voice?" the artist asked.

"It's not the drawing that has me puzzled," Angie said. "It's a very close approximation to how the man looked. But, there's something about the hair and the glasses."

"Shall we continue to work on those aspects of the face?" The artist lifted his pencil.

"It's not that." Angie frowned. "It's ... it doesn't seem right."

Chief Martin knocked and opened the door. "Is it okay if I join you two?"

The chief was waved in and he went to have a look at the artist's sketch. "Huh," he grunted.

"Why did you make that noise?" Angie asked. "Are you surprised by the drawing?"

The chief straightened and exchanged a glance with the artist.

The artist said to Chief Martin, "Angie was just telling me that it doesn't seem right."

"That's not exactly what I meant. The sketch is perfectly accurate. It looks like the man I saw at the fire." She leaned her head to the side. "Something feels wrong about his eyeglasses and his hair though."

"How do you mean?" the chief asked.

"I don't think he wears glasses, and I don't think he usually wears his hair like this."

"Why do you say that?" the artist questioned.

"Because." Angie's eyes took on a faraway expression. "I sense it. I don't think this is how he looks in real life."

"So what are you saying?" the chief was trying to decipher Angie's meaning when his eyes suddenly went wide. "Is it a disguise? Is this man doing things to himself to make him appear different than he usually does?"

Angie turned to the chief with a smile. "That's it.

A disguise. I bet he was wearing a wig. I bet he doesn't wear glasses at all. I think his mustache is false."

Earlier in the day, the salesclerk, Anna Billings, had come to the police station to meet with the artist.

"Would you show Angie the drawing you did from Ms. Billings's description?" the chief asked the artist.

The man reached into his briefcase for a second sketchbook and he flipped to the picture he'd created.

"It looks like this man could be a brother to the person I saw that night. The nose is very similar, and so are the eyes and the shape of the forehead." Angie looked up and made eye contact first with the artist, and then with Chief Martin. "He is wearing a disguise, isn't he? He wore one when Anna Billings ran into him, and he was wearing a different one when I met him. They're slight things, maybe a different wig on each of the nights. Once, he wore glasses, the other time he didn't. He had a mustache when I saw him, but he didn't have one when Anna met him."

"Clever." The chief stroked his chin. "The slight alteration in appearance is enough to throw people off, to confuse his image just enough. With the disguises, the same person is never seen at the fires so the arsonist is never identified."

Chief Martin thanked the forensic artist for his work and showed him to the door, and then he sat down next to Angie.

"Neither of these drawings look like Officer Pandy," Angie noted.

The chief covered the hair of the man in the drawing. "If I remove the hair and you think about what Pandy's hair looks like and then imagine the picture's subject with the officer's hat on his head, what do you think?"

Angie rubbed her forehead. "I guess it could be him then. Maybe. What about Pandy's son, Noah. Do you know what he looks like? Does the drawing resemble Noah?"

The chief studied the sketch and then let out a long breath of exasperation. "I've only seen the boy a few times, but yes, this could be Noah."

"What about Dave Belting, Eugene and Joan's ex-son-in-law? If we changed the hair in the picture, would it then look like Belting?"

A frown formed over the chief's face and he cursed. "The three guys resemble one another, especially if we put each man's correct hair color and hairstyle on the drawing's head. It could be any of them."

Angie rested her chin in her hand. "This didn't help much."

"Well, it did actually. It hasn't eliminated any of the men we've had in mind as suspects and the drawing doesn't look wildly different from the three." The chief looked Angie in the eye. "So it seems we could be on the right track."

"Unless there's another guy out there who also looks a whole lot like these three," Angie said.

Chief Martin groaned. "Don't even go there."

Glancing down at the drawing, Angie said, "There's something really familiar about this face. I feel like I've seen it before, and not just on the night of the fire." Raising her eyes and looking off across the room, she said, "But from where?"

22

"I hope the weather on our wedding day is as beautiful as this." Josh held Angie's hand as they walked around the grounds of the Sweet Cove Resort. When they got to the bluff, they stood looking out over the deep blue ocean and watched the waves crash on the sandy beach below them. Gulls swooped and let out cries as they floated on the air currents high above the sea. A few puffy white clouds dotted the brilliant blue sky.

"Let's keep our fingers crossed." Angie looked over her shoulder. "Here comes Lou."

Lou Michaels had worked for Josh at the resort for a couple of years as the event manager and he was meeting with Angie and Josh to go over the wedding plans. A tall, fit man in his mid-thirties,

Michaels had brown hair and brown eyes, and was always impeccably dressed.

"Hey, you two," the man called to them. "Nice to see you, Angie."

"We were just watching the waves while we were waiting," Josh said.

Angie warmly greeted their wedding planner.

Michaels had a clipboard of papers with orders and diagrams and details for the Roseland-Williams wedding. He asked Angie about the bridesmaids' dresses.

"Chosen and purchased and the shoes have been ordered," she told him. "They'll be arriving in a few days."

Michaels raised an eyebrow. "Just in time for alterations. You cut that kind of close," he chided the young woman. "Flowers?"

Angie gave a nod. "I picked them out and paid for them."

"What about your wedding dress?"

"Ellie hemmed it and is sewing any crystals, sequins, or pearls that are loose."

"Excellent. Are you still planning to make the cake?"

"Yes. When it's ready, Ellie will drive it down in her van."

"I have a note here about two cats." Michaels lifted his eyes from the notes on the clipboard. "Cats? Really?"

"They have to come," Angie said firmly.

Michaels looked to Josh for help. "How will I be able to keep track of cats?"

"They don't need to be kept track of," Angie told the man. "They're very independent."

Michaels put a hand on his hip. "What if they run off? What if they disappear or a dog comes by and attacks them? You don't want to remember your wedding day as the day your cats got killed."

"They won't run off and they won't get attacked. It will be okay. They don't cause any trouble. Most of the guests know them."

Michaels looked again to Josh for assistance. "Josh. Cats? At a wedding?"

"Euclid and Circe aren't run-of-the-mill cats," Josh said. "They're ... well, they're very special to us."

Michaels rolled his eyes. "What are they? Magic or something?" He led the way to the spot on the point where the ceremony would take place.

"Or something," Angie whispered to Josh with a smile.

"I'm putting a clause in the contract saying I'm not responsible for the welfare of the animals,"

Michaels warned. "Here." He put his arms out wide. "This is where you will say your vows. It's close to the edge of the bluff so you can hear the waves, but not too close where someone might slip and tumble down the cliff."

Angie had to bite her lip to keep from chuckling at the silly idea that someone would take a fall and disappear in the middle of the wedding.

"The arbor will be set up here," Michaels darted around like a kid in a candy store. "Flowers will be all over the arch. You'll stand right here in front of the officiant. We will have two sections of white chairs divided in the middle so that you and your attendants will be able to walk down the aisle. Flowers will be attached to the end chair and there will be two pedestals topped with large floral arrangements on either side of you." Michaels headed away. "Follow me. I'll show the bride where she will stand before making her grand entrance."

Angie and Josh followed behind.

"As we discussed, there will be valet parking for the guests and should anyone require assistance, we will have golf carts available to move them from the lot to the ceremony location." While Michaels rattled on and on about every detail, Angie started to glance around Robin's Point. Her nana had once owned a small cottage on the point where Angie and her sisters would stay for weeks in the summer until a problem with the land resulted in nana losing her little house.

Josh and his brother eventually purchased the land and had the elegant resort built. Josh met Angie, bought out his brother's ownership share, and had a lawyer draw up papers that returned most of Robin's Point to the Roseland sisters. Each one received a plot of land, but none of them had yet built on it and they weren't sure if they ever would. In two weeks, Angie and Josh would be married on the place where Nana had her cottage.

"If, heaven forbid, there is rain on that day, we will have the ceremony in one of the resort ballrooms. And not to fret, we will decorate the room and it will be fit for a princess." Michaels nodded to Josh. "And for a prince. Any questions about what will happen during outside ceremony?"

"I don't think so." Angie looked up at her fiancé and he shook his head. "Everything seems to be all set."

"Let's go inside then to the reception room." When Michaels headed for the resort buildings, Josh's phone buzzed and he had to take the call so the wedding planner went over the paperwork while Angie meandered around the point.

Whenever she and Courtney visited, they felt a soft, gentle thrumming in their blood. Courtney once told her sister that she could feel it as soon as their grandmother had passed away and that it always made her feel closer to Nana. Sometimes, when the cases they worked on with Chief Martin became too difficult, the sisters would come down to the point where they walked around, rested on the grass, or sat on the bluff to watch the ocean. Being on the point seemed to ground them and make them more receptive to the things that floated on the air.

Angie stood on the spot where the cottage used to be and she took in long, deep breaths. The arson case nagged at her. It drained her energy. Closing her eyes, Angie began to feel the familiar thrumming running through her body and she let her mind relax as the sun warmed her skin and the caw of a gull drifted towards her on the air currents.

The details of the arson case came into her mind, one by one. The victims she'd met with, the destruction and devastation wrought by the fires, the fear and anxiety in the neighbors and community members, the loving older couple, Eugene and Joan Foster, the lack of clues and evidence, the man she ran into on Main Street in Silver Cove. *I know you're the one who did it. But who are you?*

The thrumming grew more insistent and pulsed in her veins.

We'll find you. You can't hide from us forever.

Angie thought she heard a woman call her name and she opened her eyes. Looking around the lushly landscaped grounds, something caught her eye and she turned towards the movement way over on the bluff.

A woman seemed to be staring in Angie's direction. She was tall, slim, elegant. She had blond hair and fair skin.

Angie's heart stopped beating for a second and she took a step forward, blinking.

Mom?

"Ready to go inside, Angie?" Josh called to her.

Angie glanced behind her for a split-second and then quickly turned back to the woman.

She was gone.

Angie looked in every direction and when she turned her eyes to the south, the sun caught her right in the eye and blinded her for a moment causing her eyelids to slam shut.

Even though her eyes were closed, she experi-

J. A. WHITING

enced a bright red flash in her vision and felt an intense heat flare against her skin.

Angie wheeled around in a panic. *Where was Josh?*

"Are you okay?" Josh was beside her putting his arm around her shoulders.

"Yes." Angie put her fingers to her eyes. "I didn't bring my sunglasses. The sun blinded me for a second." The couple headed for the resort following the chattering wedding planner.

"There will be appetizers and drinks on the stone patio overlooking the ocean. The sun will be going down and if the day is clear, there will be a gorgeous sunset. The musicians will play instrumental selections over in the corner. There will be flowers all over. It will be stunning."

Angie could barely pay attention to the wedding planner. She knew he was the best at his job and that the wedding was going to be beautiful, but what mattered most to her was being surrounded by the people she loved and enjoying the day with them.

Standing on the patio, she took another glance to the point where the blond woman had been standing.

"Funny," Angie said to Josh with a wistful tone.

"The woman who was over there near the bluff looked just like my mother."

"A woman?" Josh asked. "I didn't see a woman there."

Michaels came up behind the couple. "There wasn't anyone there. We were the only ones on the point when we were going over the details. It must have been the sun in your eyes."

When Angie looked at Josh, a wave of anxiety and grief nearly choked her and it was as if a cold, hard hand had wrapped its icy fingers around her heart and squeezed.

23

A ngie worked at the kitchen counter next to Ellie as they cut up fruit to make a salad for part of the B and B's guest breakfasts. Eggs boiled on the stove and a coffee cake was in the oven. Yogurt, various toppings, and waffles had already been placed on the buffet table in the dining room.

"I saw a woman on Robin's Point who looked just like mom. She was a good distance from us. She was standing on the bluff."

"Did you talk to her?" Ellie asked.

"No, we were busy with the wedding planner." Angie held the knife above the honeydew melon for a few seconds before slicing. "It was funny. I told Josh the woman looked like mom, but he said he hadn't noticed a woman standing there. Lou Michaels was insistent that nobody was on the bluff when we were discussing the ceremony details."

Euclid let out a hiss from his position on top of the refrigerator.

Ellie scooped the fruit into a large cut-glass bowl. "Are you sure you saw someone? Mom has been on your mind lately with the wedding coming up and everything. Maybe you wished Mom was there. In reality, it might have been a shadow or a shaft of light that caught your attention."

Angie turned towards Ellie and stared at her. "Right after I thought I saw Mom a terrible feeling came over me. Almost a panicky sensation. I couldn't catch my breath for a few seconds. I thought Josh was in danger."

"You had quite an afternoon yesterday." Ellie teased her sister wanting to lighten the mood, but the expression on Angie's face made her change her tone. "Why do you think these things happened? Is it a reaction to stress? Is it left-over brain fog from the bad migraine you had? Is it a mixture of too many things going on? The case, running the bake shop full-time, planning a wedding."

"You make it sound like I'm losing my mind," Angie muttered.

"That's not what I mean at all. You aren't losing your mind. You've got a lot *on* your mind. Maybe it got overloaded."

"I know I could have imagined Mom on the bluff, but that thing about Josh...." She let her voice trail off. "It worries me. What if Josh is in danger?"

Ellie put her hand an Angie's arm. "I doubt he's in danger. You're about to marry him. Silly worries pop up. Josh is important to you so you want to keep him safe. And *if* he happens to be in danger, well, he's a strong, smart man and he's surrounded by all of us ... whatever it might be, we'll all handle it together."

Angie gave her sister a hug.

"Don't you need to get to the bake shop?" Ellie asked as she removed the boiled eggs from the burner.

"I took the morning off. I'm going to meet Francine in Silver Cove for a coffee. My head still feels off. I thought I'd get some paperwork done before I go to meet her, but now I think I might go back to bed for a quick nap."

Ellie said, "Go ahead. Be good to yourself over the next couple of weeks. I can finish up in here. Thanks for the help with the breakfast."

Angie finished what she was doing and then

headed for the staircase to return to her rooms. The big orange cat dashed up ahead of her and waited at the door to the apartment. Circe came around the corner to join them and when Angie opened the door, the two animals raced inside and jumped on the bed.

Angie made a cup of tea and brought it to the bedroom where she climbed under the covers and sipped the warm, soothing liquid. The cats snuggled against her and purred.

The worry she'd experienced on Robin's Point kept picking at her. Why did she feel so alarmed about Josh?

Angie remembered a red flash in her eyes. What did it mean? Did it have something to do with the arson case?

With a sigh, she put her teacup on the side table, set her alarm to go off in thirty minutes, fluffed her pillows, and closed her eyes. In just a few minutes, she had drifted off to sleep and began to dream.

The sky was a brilliant blue and the air was warm and pleasant as she walked along the busy sidewalks of Boston. She didn't remember why, but she was in a hurry. She checked her watch, and when she saw the time, she broke into a jog. Moving down the sidewalk, she dodged the pedestrians around her.

The light changed, cars raced past, and she had to stop to wait to cross the street. Her heart pounded. Sweat dripped down her temples. *Hurry up, hurry up.*

Angie took off like a rocket when the light finally changed.

When she turned the corner, her eyes searched the streets and sidewalks.

So many people.

Where is she? Where is she?

Angie saw her. The blond head bobbed along mixed in with the other people hurrying to work or to appointments or to the stores. The woman stood at the corner and when the light changed, she and several others stepped into the street to cross.

Stop, Angie yelled. *Go back. Don't cross.* She waved her arms frantically. The blonde didn't see or hear her. The woman kept walking.

The car. It ran the red light. It careened towards the woman.

Angie tried again. *Stop!*

Neither the car nor the woman stopped. Angie couldn't watch.

The car didn't brake until it was too late.

The sickening thud filled the air.

Mom.

Angie collapsed on the sidewalk. She turned her head on the concrete and looked to the blue car that had just hit her mother. It was turned at an awkward angle across the street.

People rushed forward. Some screamed.

Angie's vision dimmed and she fought to stay alert. Her eyes found the license plate of the blue car. She clearly saw the numbers and the letters, but when she blinked they began to fade.

When they'd almost disappeared, other numbers and letters took shape and filled the license plate. It was a different car. A dark sedan.

Angie stared at the license plate and memorized what she saw.

She felt soft fingers caress her forehead and she looked up from her fallen position on the Boston sidewalk, and saw the face of her mother smiling down at her.

Angie bolted up in her bed. Her shirt stuck to her back with perspiration. Her stomach clenched and her heart beat like a drum, fast and hard.

Euclid and Circe both jumped up and stared at the young woman.

"Stupid dream, stupid dream," Angie mumbled and swiped her hand across her forehead.

Then she froze.

The license plate.

Scrambling out of bed, Angie yanked open the drawer of the bedside table and fished out a pen and a small pad of pad. Her hand raced over the paper writing the license plate numbers and letters she'd seen in her dream.

The cats still stared at her.

"This is the license plate." Angie triumphantly waved the piece of paper in the air. "This is the arsonist's license plate number."

Racing out of the apartment and down the staircase, Angie bolted into the kitchen so fast that Ellie and Mr. Finch whirled around.

"I dreamt the license plate," Angie nearly yelled. "I saw the license plate in my dream."

Ellie and Finch looked at the young woman blankly.

"The arsonist's license plate. From when I bumped into him in Silver Cove." Angie hurried to her purse and pulled out her phone. "I have to call Chief Martin."

"You remembered, Miss Angie?" Finch asked.

"Yes. Chief Martin can run the numbers. He'll be able to find the car. He'll be able to find the owner."

Ellie clapped her hands. "Thank the heavens. All of this will be over."

Angie spoke to the chief and gave him the license number. She listened to his reply.

Ellie watched her sister's face, and then sidled up to Mr. Finch.

"Something isn't going the way Angie thought it would," she whispered to the older man.

Finch gripped the top of his cane and kept his voice down. "What could be wrong?"

"We'll find out in a minute," Ellie said as she wiped her hands on a dishtowel.

Angie ended the call and turned around. "Chief Martin said that Officer Pandy and his son, Noah, are coming to the station in about thirty minutes"

"Why?" Ellie took a few steps forward.

"The chief said Officer Pandy called him this morning and told him he and Noah have some information for him. Chief Martin thinks one of them is going to confess to the fires."

"That's good, isn't it?" Ellie couldn't understand why Angie didn't seem happy about it.

"I guess so." Angie placed her phone on the counter.

"Then what's wrong, Miss Angie?"

Angie lifted her eyes to Finch. "I'm not sure. Do you feel anything?"

Finch raised an eyebrow and then reached out his hand for Angie's. She stepped forward and grasped his extended hand. The two closed their eyes. For a full minute, they stood in silence.

Finch's eyelids lifted. "Is Chief Martin going to run the license number you gave him?"

"He said he would after the meeting with the Pandys. He wants to hear what they have to say first."

Euclid and Circe hissed.

Finch nodded. "Then he might discover something unexpected."

An expression of worry washed over Ellie's face. "How do you mean?"

"I don't believe the Pandys plan to tell the chief what he thinks they're going to say." Finch exchanged a look with Angie. "I think the arsonist is someone else, not one of the Pandys."

Angie nodded slowly. "But who is it?"

ngie drove Ellie's van north to Silver Cove to meet Francine for coffee, her mind buzzing with the details of the arson case. *Was one of the Pandys going to confess to setting the fires? Was it Noah who was the arsonist and his father was accompanying his son to make the confession?*

Angie didn't think it was either of the men. If she had to bet, she would say the arsonist was someone else. She wished Chief Martin would run the license plate she saw in her dream. Going to visit Francine was supposed to be a reprieve from the stress of the case, but Angie was a jumble of nerves.

And why hadn't Josh contacted her this morning? He had an early meeting in Beverly about acquiring some land for development and if he finished on time, he was going to meet her in Silver Cove at Francine's home.

Maybe his meeting ran late. Not hearing from Josh picked at her and made her feel uneasy.

Turning onto Francine's road and feeling shaky, Angie pulled to the side and stopped to compose herself, not wanting to arrive at her friend's home in a state of distress.

Taking deep breaths, she closed her eyes and tried to banish the worries from her mind. Her phone rang and Angie almost jumped out of her skin.

The phone screen indicated the caller was Joan Foster.

"Angie?" Joan asked. "Is that you?"

"Yes, Mrs. Foster. Is everything okay?" Angie could hear the nervousness in the woman's voice.

"I'm not sure. I saw the news this morning. They showed a drawing of the arson suspect. The police released the picture last night to the media."

"Yes?"

Joan nearly whispered, "It looks like our ex-son-in-law."

Angie's throat tightened.

Joan repeated what she'd said. "The drawing on

the news looks like Dave Belting. Eugene thinks so, too."

As a crushing wave of anxiety sat on Angie's chest and made it difficult to breathe, an image flashed in her vision. *Red. Smoke. The Fosters. Josh!?*

Angie's heart almost pounded through her chest. "Mrs. Foster, is my fiancé at your house?"

"What?" Joan asked with confusion in her voice.

"Never mind. I want you and your husband to leave the house. Get in your car and drive to the police station."

"Leave? I can't. We can't. Eugene had a spell this morning. He's resting in bed."

"Mrs. Foster. You need to listen to me. You *must* get out of the house now."

Before she could say another word, a roaring *boom* came over the call and Angie almost dropped the phone.

"Mrs. Foster! Joan!" Angie yelled.

Nothing.

Oh, no. Oh, no.

Angie started the engine. She was less than ten minutes away from the Fosters' house. She did a U-turn and stomped on the gas pedal

Angie didn't hear it, but a text came in from Ellie.

The cats are going berserk. Where are you? Are you okay?

When Angie approached the neighborhood, her worst fears were realized. Dark smoke rose into the sky. A few neighbors stood on the sidewalk in front of the Fosters' house. Screeching to a halt, Angie jumped out of the van, and then she saw Josh's car parked askew on the side of the road.

Angie ran to the people on the sidewalk. She could see the flames rising from the back of the house.

"Did the Fosters get out?" Angie asked frantically.

"We don't think so." A woman had tears in her eyes.

"Did anyone call the fire department?" Angie took some steps towards the house scanning for Josh.

"Yes."

One of the neighbors spoke. "A man ran inside. That's his car over there. He jumped out, saw the fire, and ran through the front door."

Angie's heart almost stopped and for a few seconds, she couldn't breathe.

Josh.

Ripping her sweater off planning to hold it to her

nose once inside, she took off running for the front porch.

Josh is inside.

Angie grabbed the doorknob. It was warm to the touch. She turned it without hesitation and stepped into the inferno.

Smoke filled the living room.

The fire raged at the back of the house, crackling, hissing, booming.

The interior walls showed crimson, reflecting the flames.

Holding her sweater to her nose, Angie hunched down and moved forward. She screamed for Josh even though she knew he wouldn't be able to hear her over the furious din of the blazing fire.

Joan said Eugene was resting in bed so Angie approached the hallway to the bedrooms. The family room and kitchen at the rear of the house were fully engulfed.

She put her hand on the hallway wall and gingerly moved her feet. The smoke was so heavy that she couldn't see further than five inches in front of her face.

Angie felt like she was walking through hell. She knew she would die in that house, but she had to find Josh. When tears tried to form in her eyes, the moisture was sucked away in the heat.

A coughing fit started just as her toe hit something on the floor.

Angie bent and felt around until she touched flesh. A man's thick arm. *Eugene.*

Someone bumped into her. She stood straight still holding the sweater to her nose.

"Angie!"

It was Josh carrying Mrs. Foster. Angie's heart leapt.

Putting his face close to his fiancee's ear, Josh yelled as he attempted to put Mrs. Foster into Angie's arms. "Take her. Can you carry her? Go! I'll carry Eugene."

Josh placed Joan over Angie's shoulder and despite the weight, Angie's body surged with so much energy, she carried the woman without trouble.

Angie turned and used her hand to follow the wall back into the living room. Unable to see anything, she used her senses to make it to the front door. Just as she reached it, she thought she could hear sirens.

From behind her, a deafening crash smashed into Angie's eardrums.

She opened the door and carefully laid Mrs. Foster on the porch ... and then she went back inside.

Later, she would be told that the crashing sound was part of the roof collapsing into the home's hallway.

Angie crawled on her hands and knees through the smoke, feeling with her hands for Josh.

Her fingers hit Eugene's head.

"My legs," Josh moaned weakly. "Get Eugene out of here. Get out of here, Angie."

Angie hunched and grabbed the older man's wrists, and with all of her might, she dragged him to the front door, and then rushed back for Josh.

"Get out," Josh told Angie weakly. "Leave me. Please go. I love you, Angie. Don't you dare die in here."

"I am not ... leaving you," Angie gasped, completely exhausted. Slipping her hands under Josh's armpits, she dragged her fiancé forward, little by little, and just as they cleared the hall, the space went up in a roar of flames.

Angie fell onto her back.

It's too hard. I can't do it.

Barely able to breathe, Angie gave up hope ... and then she heard her mother's voice in her head.

239

Get up. Save Josh. Pull Josh out. Get out. Do it, Angie. Go now.

Angie pushed herself up, crawled forward again, took hold of Josh's hands, stood hunched over, and dragged him, inch by miserable inch to the door.

When she collapsed onto the front porch, she fainted, but it didn't matter. She was met there by the firefighters who carried her and Josh to safety.

ANGIE'S EYES blinked open to see the blue, cloudless sky above her and for a moment, she thought she was on a blanket on the white sandy beach of Sweet Cove.

There was some kind of plastic thing over her nose and mouth, and then she remembered.

She sat up on the stretcher and lifted the oxygen mask from her nose.

An EMT was next to her. "You're okay. Hold on there. Don't get up."

"Where's Josh?" Angie heart banged in her chest. "Where's my Josh?"

"He's going to be fine," the man said to her as he adjusted the oxygen mask. "Rest back on the stretcher."

"Where is he?" Angie leaned against the EMT trying not to let him push her into reclining position. "Where's Josh?"

Angie heard her sisters' voices calling to her and in a moment, she was rushed by Jenna, Ellie, and Courtney who hugged her, clucked over her, and with tears running down their faces, told her they loved her.

"Please tell me Josh is alive." Tears rolled down Angie's soot-covered face.

"He's alive, Miss Angie." Mr. Finch wrapped his arms around the young woman and for a moment, placed his head against her chest. "Thank the heavens. And so are you," he whispered. "You're still here with us. I was so afraid." He lifted his head and tears glistened on his cheeks. "You're still here with us."

"I could kill you," Courtney said sternly. "You ran into a burning house. It was a stupid, stupid thing to do." The honey-blonde pushed her tears away with both palms. "But, I would have done it for you."

Angie reached out to hold her youngest sister's hand. "I'm sorry. But I had to."

"Josh has been taken to the hospital," Mr. Finch informed the group. "It appears he may have broken his leg." The older man leaned on his cane and smiled at the woman on the stretcher. "But the rest of him is just fine and dandy."

Suddenly, Angie lifted her head with worried eyes. "The Fosters. Are they...?"

"They're alive," Jenna said. "Banged up and a little worse for the wear, but you and Josh saved them. They're on the way to the hospital."

"And that's where we're taking you now," the EMT said to Angie and when he rolled the stretcher to the waiting ambulance, she turned her head to see the Fosters' house fully engulfed in angry flames that were reaching up to the sky.

25

A ngie, three of her sisters, the cats, Mr. Finch, Tom, Rufus, Betty, Chief Martin and his wife, Lucille, sat in chairs under the pergola. Burgers, veggie burgers, and hot dogs cooked on the grill and the smell of the food made Angie's stomach growl.

Drinking an iced tea, Josh sat in a wheelchair with his left leg in a cast and a big black boot on his broken right foot. The injuries occurred when part of the roof caved in and collapsed on top of Josh. He was able to use crutches once in a while, but the orthopedist wanted him to stay off of the legs for a while. Circe rested on the man's lap.

"It's actually not that bad with everyone waiting on me," Josh said.

"Don't get used to it," Courtney told her soon-to-be-brother-in-law while handing him a plate with some appetizers.

Tom had quickly constructed a ramp to the back door so it would be easy to move Josh in and out of the Victorian. The house had two handicap accessible rooms on the first floor so the family installed Josh into one of them.

Angie had been discharged from the hospital after being treated for smoke inhalation, a few burns on her arms, and various cuts, one that required several stitches. Josh stayed over in the hospital for two nights and was then released.

The Fosters' health issues kept them in the hospital longer, but they'd recently been released to a rehab center, and in about a week the couple would be allowed to return to Silver Cove where they planned to rent a townhouse.

The license plate number Angie had sent the chief turned out to belong to Dave Belting, the former son-in-law of the Fosters.

When the police arrived at his mother's house to bring him in, Belting was not at home nor was he at work. The man was busy setting one last fire.

Joan and Eugene reported that Dave arrived on their doorstep the night before he set fire to their home. Dave asked the couple for a loan, but when they told him they could only spare half of what he wanted, he became angry, ranted for a minute, then quickly left the house.

Dave had told the Fosters that he wanted to get away from Silver Cove to start a new life, but that he lacked the necessary funds. When he arrived at the house, he was disheveled and smelled strongly of alcohol. He wasn't violent towards Joan or Eugene and he was able to converse coherently so the couple decided there was no reason to alert the police to the unexpected visit.

When the Fosters saw the police sketch of the suspect on the morning news, they panicked and called Angie planning to ask her if their worries were foolish or should they contact the police. The conversation never got that far.

Found wandering around in the center of Silver Cove, Dave Belting was picked up by police and arrested for arson and was also charged with counts of first degree murder for the people killed in one of the fires.

Police learned that Dave had started setting fires when he was eight-years-old. He was a difficult young man and he was a pathological liar who delighted in seeing firefighters working at a scene. In the basement of his home, the police found various wigs, fake moustaches and beards, different kinds of eyeglasses, hats, and temporary tattoos ... as well as empty bottles of High Star beer. Dave Belting had clearly mastered the art of disguise. The police also learned from cell phone records that Dave's phone was in the vicinity when many of the fires had been set.

The Fosters, kindhearted and forgiving, felt sorry for Dave and for the man's lifelong troubles and struggles.

Josh had harsh words for his sweetheart and her foolhardy entrance into a burning building.

Angie told him, "I'm going to ignore your comments since you did the very same thing to save the Fosters before I arrived at the house."

Josh had left his meeting in Beverly and was almost to Francine's house when he saw the dark smoke in the sky rising from the east. He drove to see if there was trouble, saw the Fosters' home on fire, and darted inside to help the couple to safety. The fire moved quickly and the place filled with smoke and flames so fast that Josh couldn't get them out before the house went up like a dried-out piece of wood.

"You should have left me," Josh had said to Angie

while in the hospital. "I couldn't bear to think I might be the cause of your death."

"Then in the future, don't run into burning buildings," Angie held his eyes with hers. "Because I *will* go in after you."

Josh said, "I told Joan to get out when I was trying to get Eugene out of his bed. She wouldn't budge. She said she wasn't leaving without her husband and if that meant they both died in the blaze, then they would go together."

"Sounds a lot like you and me," Angie smiled.

Josh reached for her hand. "It sounds a lot like love and devotion."

BETTY FILLED her drink from the pitcher of iced tea on the table under the pergola and asked Chief Martin, "What did the Pandys say to you that morning? Obviously, they didn't want to confess to the fires."

Chief Martin swallowed his bite of mushroom turnover. "Officer Pandy and his son wanted to talk to me about something Noah saw on one of the nights of a fire. He was in the neighborhood visiting a friend and when he left and was walking to the center of town to get a pizza, he noticed someone hurrying away from the area. The man had a strange smile on his face, smelled of alcohol, and had a weird, wild look in his eyes."

Noah didn't think much of it, but the man popped into his head later when he learned about the fires and finally decided to bring it up with his father.

Officer Pandy thought it was best to bring the information to the attention of investigators. Noah thought he had recognized the man. He told Chief Martin the man might be Dave Belting.

When they were there to interview the older couple, Angie had seen a wedding picture of a woman and Dave Belting on the table of photographs in the Fosters' living room. At the time, she didn't know it was Dave, but when she bumped into the man at the Main Street fire, the reason he seemed familiar was because she'd seen his photo at Joan's and Eugene's home.

She knew she'd seen the arsonist before, she just could not place where it had been.

Jenna said, "When I came into the kitchen before going to my jewelry shop, the cats were howling and running through the house like a couple of lunatics. When Ellie or I tried to shush them, they hissed at us with arched backs and started running through the house, stopping at the doors jumping at the doorknobs. We knew something bad was happening."

Angie smiled at Euclid and Circe. "Good ones. You knew Josh and I were in trouble. You alerted Ellie and Jenna. Thank you."

The two fine felines purred at the compliments they'd received.

When Tom got up to check the grill, Mr. Finch looked at his watch. "Miss Ellie should have been back by now."

As if on cue, Jack, wearing a pressed shirt, blazer, and green bowtie, came down the driveway and walked into the yard to greet the group.

Angie stood up with a concerned look on her face. "Where's Ellie?"

"Well, Ellie didn't want to come back right away," Jack said solemnly.

"What?" Courtney said loudly. "She didn't get it? That's outrageous. I don't believe it."

Jack's face broke into a smile.

"You're right not to believe it." Ellie came around the corner wearing a light blue business suit and a bright smile. "We didn't come back right away because we stopped for this." A bottle of champagne was in her hand. "It's time to celebrate."

"You *did* get it." Courtney hugged her sister. "Congratulations. We knew you'd get it."

"Hooray!" Mr. Finch stood up, beamed at the young woman, and addressed the family and friends. "May I take this moment to introduce to you the newest member of the Sweet Cove town finance committee."

A cheer went up from the group and everyone, except Josh, rushed forward to give Ellie their congratulations.

"It was great," Ellie told them. "I didn't feel calm, but I was able to project confidence and I answered all of their questions well. I was happy with my interview and no matter what they decided I was pleased that I'd done what I could."

"And it was more than excellent." Jack put his arm around Ellie's shoulders.

Josh called to the tall blonde and asked her to come over so he could give her a hug. "I'm sort of incapacitated," he chuckled when Ellie walked over to him.

"You need an air horn or a cow bell to get people's attention," Ellie said.

Courtney rolled her eyes. "Gosh. He's already

being waited on hand and foot. He's really milking this. Don't give him any ideas."

Angie came out of the house carrying a three-layer cake with chocolate toffee frosting. She placed it on the long wooden table. On the top, the word, *Congratulations*, was written in frosting.

"It's beautiful." Ellie hugged her oldest sister. "But what if I didn't get the finance board seat?"

Angie laughed. "Then we would have scraped off the *Congratulations* and eaten it anyway."

Tom and Rufus removed the food from the grill and placed it on platters while Ellie and Jack poured champagne and delivered the glasses to everyone.

The sun was low in the sky and the backyard lights and torches were lit casting a golden glow around the garden.

Jack proposed a toast to Ellie and her success and everyone clapped and hooted while the cats trilled.

When Ellie raised her glass, she said, "I'm feeling very lucky."

Angie went over to Josh and when she clinked her glass to his, he looked lovingly into her eyes. "I'm feeling the very same way."

26

The sky was as blue and clear as if someone painted the perfection way up on the atmosphere ... or as if someone wished it and the wish came true.

Euclid had a miniature black bow tie at his neck, his orange ruff of fur threatening to cover it up. Circe had on a lavender ribbon tied in a pretty bow.

The cats watched as Angie put some finishing touches of frosting on the tiers of the wedding cake.

She put the tube of frosting on the kitchen counter. "There. It's done. I'll just add a little more when I get to the resort."

"I thought you'd be stressed out by making your own wedding cake before getting ready to walk down the aisle," Ellie said.

"I am stressed out." Angie smiled. "But it's all relative. This kind of stress is nothing compared to being inside a burning house trying to save the person you love."

"I can't believe what you just said actually happened." Ellie shook her head. "I'll never make it to old age. You're all going to shorten my life making me worry about you."

Angie gave her sister a friendly bop and teased. "Aren't you used to it yet?"

"I won't even answer that." Ellie looked at the clock. "Shouldn't you be getting dressed?"

Jenna and Courtney came into the kitchen wearing their lavender bridesmaids' dresses. Their hair had been blow-dried and gently curled at the bottom. Their makeup was subtle and elegant.

Angie stared at the two of them and sighed. "Wow."

After admiring the cake, the sisters went upstairs to help Angie with her hair and makeup, and then into her dress. The cats sat on the bed to watch.

"Euclid isn't even fussing about wearing a tie," Courtney noted.

"It's his third wedding. He must be used to it by now," Jenna said as she swept Angie's hair into a low chignon. "There." The final pin was placed. "It looks terrific."

When Courtney left to help the men with their boutonnieres, Ellie took the wedding gown off the hangar and held it out for Angie to slip on.

Jenna zipped it up.

The dress fit perfectly, and the little pearls and tiny sequins caught the light and shimmered.

"Are you doing okay?" Ellie asked. "I know you've been missing Mom."

"I'm good." Angie smiled. "Even though Mom never appears, I know she's here with us. She's helped me over the past few weeks."

"Mom never was comfortable with the whole paranormal thing," Jenna said. "So maybe showing up as a ghost doesn't appeal to her ... but I think she's found her own way to be close to us."

Angie nodded.

"The car is here for you," Courtney called up the stairs to Angie.

Angie moved gracefully down the staircase to the foyer where Mr. Finch, in his tuxedo, with tears trickling in little streams down his cheeks, waited to escort her to the resort. "You are a vision, Miss Angie."

Jenna handed her sister the bouquet of flowers.

As Courtney passed by on her way outside, she handed Finch a tissue and teased, "There's a whole case waiting for you at the resort, Mr. Finch."

Dabbing at his cheeks, Finch said, "I never knew the blessings of family until I met all of you. I am most grateful."

"We're the ones who are grateful to have you in our lives, Mr. Finch." Angie hugged the man tightly, then took his hand in hers and led him out of the Victorian to the red convertible roadster that Josh had sent for them.

Riding down the streets of Sweet Cove to the wedding venue, Angie's and Finch's giggles could be heard ringing out as the breeze blew gently against them on the way to the resort. "What a delight," Finch squealed.

Lou Michaels was waiting at the front of the resort and when the car swooped in, he rushed forward to open the car door for Angie. "Perfection, that's what you are. Now come along. The guests have taken their seats."

"Already? It's time?" Angie asked, nervousness bubbling up inside of her.

"No time like the present. It's rude to keep guests

waiting." Michaels gently moved Finch next to Angie and she slipped her hand through the man's arm.

"Where are my sisters and the men?" Angie asked nervously.

"They are in their positions. Follow me." Michaels led the bride and her escort out to Robin's Point where the guests sat in rows of white chairs. Flowers overflowed in baskets and vases on pedestals, blooms were attached to backs of the chairs, and fragrant flowering vines wound around the arbor.

The cats sat on cushions near the front row.

The wonderful aroma of the blooms floated on the air and Angie sniffed the sweet smell.

Courtney, Ellie, and Jenna waited in line for their sister to get into position and when everything was ready, the quartet began to play.

The men, handsome in their tuxedos, entered from the side and moved slowly to the front, next to the arbor. Jack, Rufus, and Josh's brother led the way followed by Josh in his wheelchair being pushed by Tom. Josh was helped to his feet and handed his crutches.

After the sisters walked down the aisle, Angie

and Mr. Finch proceeded to step slowly and elegantly towards the arbor, nodding and smiling at the guests.

Angie looked like a princess in her gorgeous gown, and Josh moved his hand over his watery eyes as she came close.

Finch kissed the young woman's cheek, shook hands with Josh, and took his seat next to his girl-friend, Betty.

"You look very handsome, Victor," Betty cooed to Finch and kissed him.

Angie beamed at her soon-to-be-husband. "Ready?"

Josh's eyes were full of love. "I've waited a long time to say these words to you."

Angie put her arm around Josh's waist and the justice of the peace started the ceremony. Vows were spoken and rings were exchanged in the sweet, simple rites of marriage, and when the music began again, Angie helped Josh into the wheelchair and pushed him up the aisle with Euclid and Circe sitting on his lap.

Everyone enjoyed drinks and conversation on the stone patio overlooking the ocean, and then moved inside for dinner.

When it was time for Angie's and Josh's first

dance, Angie sat gently on her husband's lap and put her arms around his neck while Josh used his hands to move the wheelchair to the music.

"Not exactly how I envisioned our wedding dance," Josh said with a wink. "But we're making it work."

"As long as we're together, that's the only thing that matters." Angie touched Josh's cheek.

The music kicked into high gear and the family and friends took to the dance floor to join the happy couple. Finch, holding his cane in one hand and Betty's in his other, swayed and gyrated to the beat, perspiration beading on his forehead.

Jenna and Tom, Courtney and Rufus, and Ellie and Jack moved over the wooden floor dancing and whooping it up. Friends joined in, too ... Francine and her boyfriend, Angie's hairstylist, Gloria, and her husband, Mel and Orla Able, Chief Martin and Lucille, Louisa and Lance, and other friends from town and some others from Boston. Even Joan and Eugene Foster danced to two songs.

Josh and Angie went out to the patio for a breather and sat together looking at the moon and the stars twinkling overhead in the inky sky. The waves crashed against the beach below the bluff.

Euclid and Circe sat on the small stonewall encircling the patio.

"Are you feeling comfortable?" Angie asked. "Are you tired?"

"A little tired, but going on adrenaline," Josh smiled. "The doctor told me it's normal to feel tired as the body works to heal its breaks and injuries. I'm having a wonderful time. It's been a perfect day. Are you doing okay?"

"I feel great. I couldn't have dreamed a more perfect wedding day."

"It almost didn't happen." Josh's face took on a serious expression and he took in a long breath.

"*Almost* doesn't count," Angie told him.

"Sometimes being in the fire jumps into my head and I panic a little." Josh squeezed Angie's hand. "Sometimes I dream about it ... and in the dream, we don't get out."

"But we did get out. And here we are."

"Do you think about it sometimes? Do you get frightened by the thoughts of what might have been?" Josh asked.

Angie nodded. "Sometimes when I smell a bit of smoke, or I feel a rush of heat from the oven, or I hear a smashing sound, I break out in a cold sweat. I want to run. My heart races. I have to tell myself it isn't happening. I'm safe. There's no fire. You aren't trapped in the building."

"I do the same. Talk to myself until the panic passes. Sometimes, it takes a long time to calm down."

"That day, when I couldn't move you and the fire was raging around us, I gave up. I could barely breathe. I could hardly see. I lost hope and I just lay there on my back waiting for the end to happen." Angie swallowed hard. "Then I heard my mother's voice in my mind. She told me to get up, to pull you out, to keep going, to not give up."

Angie looked out over the dark sea. "You know which of my mother's words made me find the strength to get out? *Save Josh.* I couldn't muster the energy to move. I had nothing left. Nothing. But when those words played in my head, *pull Josh out,* I knew I had to get you out of there. If it was the last thing I ever did, I had to get you outside. And somehow I made myself move. I couldn't find any strength inside me until I thought of you. *You* got us out of there. I couldn't have done it without you."

Josh took her hands in his. "Thank you for loving me, Angie. Thank you for saving us."

Angie put her hands on the sides of Josh's face, looked deeply into his eyes, and then leaned in and kissed him ... her beloved husband ... with the sound of the waves in the distance, the light warm breeze against their skin, and with the stars shining down.

And with two fine felines watching over them.

THANK YOU FOR READING! RECIPES BELOW!

Books by J.A. WHITING can be found here:
www.amazon.com/author/jawhiting

To hear about new books and book sales, please sign up for my mailing list at:
www.jawhitingbooks.com

Your email will never be sold, shared, or spammed.

If you enjoyed the book, please consider leaving a review. A few words are all that's needed. It would be very much appreciated.

BOOKS/SERIES BY J. A. WHITING

CLAIRE ROLLINS COZY MYSTERY SERIES

PAXTON PARK COZY MYSTERIES

LIN COFFIN COZY MYSTERY SERIES

SWEET COVE COZY MYSTERY SERIES

OLIVIA MILLER MYSTERY-THRILLER SERIES
(not cozy)

ABOUT THE AUTHOR

J.A. Whiting lives with her family in New England. Whiting loves reading and writing mystery stories.

Visit me at:

www.jawhitingbooks.com

www.bookbub.com/authors/j-a-whiting

www.amazon.com/author/jawhiting

www.facebook.com/jawhitingauthor

SOME RECIPES FROM THE SWEET COVE SERIES

EASY BAKLAVA

INGREDIENTS

1 pound chopped nuts (I use half walnuts and half almonds)

1½ teaspoons ground cinnamon

1 16-ounce package phyllo dough

1 cup butter, melted

1 cup granulated sugar

1 cup water

¾ cup honey

1½ teaspoons vanilla extract

1 teaspoon grated lemon or orange zest

DIRECTIONS

Preheat the oven to 350 degrees F.

Grease a 9 X 13 inch baking dish.

Mix together nuts and cinnamon.

Unroll phyllo dough – cut the stack in half; cover with damp cloth.

Put three sheets of phyllo in the bottom of the greased dish and brush with butter.

Sprinkle 2-3 teaspoons of nut mixture on top of the phyllo.

Repeat the layers until all ingredients are used; use 5-6 sheets of phyllo for the top layer.

Use a sharp knife to cut baklava into four long rows (cut all the way to the bottom of dish); then cut diagonally nine times to make 36 diamond-shaped pieces.

Bake for about 50 minutes in preheated oven or until the baklava is crisp and golden in color.

Next, combine sugar and water in a small to medium saucepan and over medium heat, bring to a boil; stir in the honey, vanilla, and lemon or orange zest – reduce heat and simmer for about 20 minutes.

Remove baklava from oven and spoon the syrup over it.

Let cool before serving.

COCOA CREAM PIE

INGREDIENTS

½ cup unsweetened cocoa powder

½ cup all-purpose flour

3 egg yolks

1¼ cups sugar

¼ teaspoon salt

2 cups milk

1½ teaspoons vanilla

Prebaked pie shell

Whipped Cream for the top of the pie

DIRECTIONS

Mix cocoa, flour, beaten egg yolks, sugar, and salt and put into a medium-sized sauce pan.

Add milk gradually to the mixture while stirring over medium-high heat until thick and smooth (it can take up to 15 minutes for the mixture to thicken).

Pour into a prebaked pie shell (your own favorite recipe or a store-bought shell).

Place in the refrigerator to chill.

Finish with whipped cream over the top and enjoy !

CHOCOLATE DING DONGS

INGREDIENTS FOR CAKES

   2 ounces semisweet chocolate

   1 cup hot brewed coffee

   2 cups granulated sugar

   1⅔ cups all-purpose flour

   1 cup unsweetened cocoa powder

   1⅓ teaspoons baking soda

   ½ teaspoon baking powder

   ¾ teaspoon salt

   2 large eggs

   ½ cup vegetable oil

   1 cup buttermilk (shake well)

   ¾ teaspoons vanilla extract

DIRECTIONS FOR CAKES

Preheat the oven to 350 degrees F.

Grease bottoms of 2 10-inch round cake pans; line each with wax paper; grease wax paper.

Chop chocolate finely; place in mixing bowl.

Pour hot coffee over chocolate; allow the mixture to stand and wait until chocolate is melted; stir now and then; when chocolate is melted, stir until smooth.

In a large bowl, sift together sugar, flour, cocoa powder, baking soda, baking powder, and salt.

In a different bowl, use an electric mixture to beat eggs; slowly add in oil, buttermilk, vanilla, and melted chocolate mixture to eggs; beat to combine well; add sugar mixture and beat on medium speed until combined.

Divide batter between the two prepared pans; bake for about one hour (a toothpick should come out clean when inserted into the center).

Cool layers.

Use a thin knife to run around the edges of the pans; invert the cake layers onto racks and cool; gently remove the wax paper; cool completely.

INGREDIENTS FOR FILLING

1 cup sugar plus 2 more tablespoons

3 large egg whites

¼ teaspoon cream of tartar

⅛ teaspoon salt

1¼ tablespoons vanilla extract

DIRECTIONS FOR FILLING

In large metal bowl, whisk together ⅓ cup water, sugar, egg whites, cream of tartar, and salt.

Set bowl over pan of gently simmering water; mix with hand-held electric mixer – low speed; slowly increase speed to high and beat until mixture can hold stiff peaks.

Move the bowl from the pan to set on a towel on the counter; continue beating until mixture is smooth (about 2-3 minutes).

Beat in vanilla.

INGREDIENTS FOR GANACHE

14 ounces semisweet chocolate, chop into ½ ounce pieces

1 cup heavy cream

1 tablespoon unsalted butter

DIRECTIONS FOR GANACHE

Place chocolate pieces into a stainless steel bowl.

In small saucepan, bring the cream to boil; remove from heat; pour cream over the chocolate.

Let mixture stand for 4-5 minutes, then stir until smooth and well-combined.

TO PUT IT TOGETHER

Use small round cookie cutter to cut small circles of cake from the two layers.

Use a teaspoon to scoop out a small portion of the cake from each circle and set it aside.

Fill with prepared filling and replace the cut-out hole.

Use a spoon to cover each individual cake with ganache; let ganache set before serving.

VANILLA CAKE WITH CHOCOLATE TOFFEE FROSTING

INGREDIENTS FOR CAKE

½ cup butter

½ cup packed brown sugar

2 cups finely crushed vanilla wafers

2 cups finely chopped pecans (leave out if allergic or don't care for nuts)

1 cup butter

1½ cups packed dark brown sugar

¾ cup granulated sugar

4 large eggs

2½ cups all-purpose flour

2 teaspoons baking powder

½ teaspoon salt

¼ teaspoon baking soda

1 8-ounce container sour cream

½ cup buttermilk

2 teaspoons vanilla extract

INGREDIENTS FOR FROSTING

1 cup semisweet chocolate chips

½ cup heavy cream

¾ cup butter

6 cups powdered sugar

1 cup chocolate covered toffee bars

DIRECTIONS FOR CAKE

Preheat the oven to 350 degrees F.

In bowl, stir together ½ cup melted butter and brown sugar; add vanilla wafers and nuts (if desired); mix well.

Spread mixture into greased baking pan.

Bake 15-20 minutes; stir once after about 10 minutes; cool.

Beat butter at medium speed until creamy; gradually add in dark brown sugar and granulated sugar, beat well; add egg yolks one at a time, beat until blended.

Stir together flour, baking powder, salt, and baking soda.

In a separate bowl, stir together sour cream, buttermilk, and vanilla.

Alternate adding flour mixture and then sour cream mixture to butter mixture; after each addition, beat at low speed to blend.

Beat (high speed) egg whites in a separate bowl until peaks form.

Gently stir ⅓ of egg whites into the batter and then fold in the remaining egg whites.

Grease and flour 3 nine-inch cake pans; line with parchment paper.

Sprinkle 1 cup of vanilla wafer mixture into the bottom of each pan.

Spoon batter into prepared pans.

Bake 18-20 minutes or until a toothpick inserted into the center comes out clean.

Cool in pans for 10 minutes; remove cakes from pans; cool for another hour.

DIRECTIONS FOR FROSTING

Using a microwave-safe bowl, microwave chocolate chips and ¼ cup cream at medium power for 2-3 minutes until melted and smooth; stirring every 30 seconds; cool to room temperature.

At medium speed, beat softened butter until creamy; gradually add in powdered sugar and remaining ¼ cup cream.

Beat in chocolate mixture until fluffy.

Spread frosting between the cake layers, on top, and on sides of cake.

Stir together remaining vanilla wafer mixture and the chopped toffee bars; press on the sides of the cake.

Serve !

54872269R00175

Made in the USA
San Bernardino,
CA